DARK WATERS

CELTIC LEGACY BOOK 1

SHANNON MAYER

HiJinks

Celtic Legacy Book I

Shannon Mayer

Electronic Edition

Created with Vellum

ACKNOWLEDGMENTS

To those with siblings, be they of blood or chosen family. We may fight against one another for the last cookie. We may fight against one another for attention. We may fight one another for the sake of fighting.

But when it comes to fighting for one another, to saving one from the darkness, there are no people more truly willing to lose it all to save us than our siblings.

And for you, this book was written.

PROLOGUE

Courage is resistance to fear, mastery of fear, not absence of fear.

1

The Eric Martin Pavilion was a nuthouse. A nice nuthouse, in the very nice town of Victoria, on Vancouver Island, but still, that fact didn't change what the place was, nor did it change the fact that it held people behind locked doors.

We weren't the only visitors going in, there were other families here to visit their loved ones. All the visitors had a certain look to them, one that I was sure I had on my face too. Happy on the surface, but resignation in their eyes. Seeing someone you loved when they were no longer themselves, was in a word, hard.

"Do you think Grandpa will know us today?" Ashling asked. Her strawberry blond curls were held back in a bouncy ponytail, and her wide green eyes—just like Mom's—had a look of perpetual surprise—also just like Mom's. Younger than me by a couple of years, she didn't have as many memories of our grandfather as I did. There was less for her to have lost in a way, by not realizing all that was gone.

But I remembered. His laughter, his tractor rides, the time he spent showing me how to tie knots for my girl scout troop. He was the only male figure in my life, and he'd . . .well he'd disappeared too in his own way.

"I hope so," I said as we stepped through the main entrance and headed down the long hall. I gave a quick wave to the nurse at the desk and she buzzed us through a double set of glass doors. The smell of antiseptic and the fainter underlying smell of body fluids made my throat tighten. Grandpa didn't deserve to be in here, not really.

We paused at an intersection to let two attendants pass; a patient held up between them. The patient hung forward, allowing the attendants to carry most of his weight, his feet dragging behind. We were still in the minimum-security section, nowhere near the people who were kept really locked up or drugged. Basically, that meant there were no really dangerous people—just those that had lost touch with reality. Like Grandpa. My heart gave a pang and I could almost hear him, his advice something I leaned on more often than not.

"It'll be okay, Quinn, no matter what the world throws at you, you just keep moving forward. If your story isn't over, it's not the end, and you'll see. Life has a funny way of working out."

"I, I, I, I don't, want, want, want a bath. I'm melting, melting!" The patient hanging between the two orderlies screamed as the odd threesome disappeared around a far corner. He ended with a fair imitation of a witch's cackle that made my lips twitch.

Ashling wasn't so subtle and let out a giggle. I bit the inside of my cheek to stop from grinning. Laughing at the people in here wasn't only unkind, but it wasn't fair. They didn't know where they were half the time, at least from those I'd seen. And many of them were here for the same reason Grandpa was—their inability to adjust to reality and deal with what was inside their heads. But sometimes, even knowing that, it was hard not to be amused by the things they said and did, seeing the very small silver lining in the darkness of being stuck here.

I cleared my throat into my hand. "You shouldn't laugh, Ash. It isn't nice."

Her mirth was wiped away in an instant and her eyes narrowed. "Shut up, Quinn. You aren't Mom. You can't tell me what to do."

My jaw clenched in a sudden reflex that I struggled to quell. Really, I was struggling not to give her a smack upside the back of her head. I mean, she was right, I wasn't her mother. Yet, I might as well have been for all the time Mom took for Ashling for the first eighteen years of her life. Recently Ash had taken to reminding me I had no say in what she did, or who she did it with. It irritated me and she knew it.

Our relationship as sisters was to say the least, a bit complicated.

I kept my eyes forward, pretending as though her sharp snap at me hadn't hurt my feelings, as if it didn't bother me at all.

Grandpa was at the far side of the facility, which meant that we passed a lot of doors. The sounds filling the Eric Martin Pavilion were a series of voices, gasps, groans and even the occasional screech.

"I hate that Grandpa's here. He doesn't belong with these crazies," Ashling's voice quivered as we passed a particularly bad screamer, one that threw himself at the door over and over again, banging his head against the wooden door.

"Get me out of here! They're using me as a test monkey! I'm human, not a monkey!" He screamed. His eyes locked on us and I made the mistake of making eye contact.

His pupils were pinpricks in the green orbs, and his mouth moved silently as he followed us in the only way he could with his head pressed against the small plastic square. It took everything I had to break eye contact with him, and the moment left me shaken more than I wanted to admit.

I reached out for Ash's hand and, for the first time in a long time, she took it, her petite fingers wrapping around mine.

"I hate it here too," I said.

One more turn and we were at our destination.

We stood in front of Grandpa's room, his door ajar and the smell of coffee rolling out of it which was a bit of a shock. I wasn't sure he was even allowed coffee in here. The nameplate read *Blake Lorkan*, though they'd misspelled it, using a k instead of a c in Lorcan. He was one of the patients allowed to wander the pavilion, perfectly safe, just totally unable to connect reality with well, with reality. None of the anti-psychotics, sedatives, or whatever else the doctors had tried had worked for him, none of them had brought back the grandpa I remembered and loved.

When you love something let it go, and if it be loving you back, then you'll find your way together again. That's how the heart is.

I only wish that part of Grandpa's advice had held true. He was gone, and he was never coming back. My throat tightened as I stood there outside his door. Neither I nor Ashling were really in a hurry to go into his room, if her lack of movement was any indicator.

Grandpa was trapped inside his head, and the monsters that haunted him there had gotten him into trouble more than once in the real world. He'd tried attacking a couple of cars, believing that they were dragons. To be fair they'd been spitting out a lot of black smoke, but the owners hadn't been too happy when he'd shot their engines full of holes with his shotgun.

Mom had considered putting him in an old folk's home, but he was still too young for that—too healthy and with too much energy. He was barely sixty, not old at all. So, the Eric Martin

Pavilion Mental Institute it was for the man who was the closest thing to a father we had.

I steeled my nerves and pushed the door open, then peeked inside. Grandpa sat in his chair, staring out the window with a cup of coffee clutched between his hands, the muscles in his arms tensed.

"Grandpa!" Ashling called out as she dashed past me and into the room, as if to make up for the fact that she'd hesitated. She threw her arms around his neck.

I don't think she noticed, but I saw him jump when she spoke, shudder when she gave him a hug. He didn't put the coffee mug down. She let him go and stepped back, smoothing her hair repeatedly. "Grandpa, did you miss us?"

My heart panged.

He tipped his head and stared at Ashling, and his eyes went distant as he looked through her. As if she weren't even there. "Hello? Who be here?" The faintest of Irish accents was still on his tongue from his early years growing up on the Green Isle. A lifetime ago, but it was his heritage—and ours.

Ashling's face fell and she dropped to her knees in front of him, carefully putting her hands on his knees. She had always been the sweetheart, the good girl, the one that was spoiled beyond all spoiling.

"Grandpa, it's me, Ashling. I came to visit you," she said, her hands reaching out to take away his coffee mug and set it on the table. When she went to take his hands in hers, he pulled his fingers away from her, slowly bringing them to his chest. A twist on his lips as though he'd smelled something awful only added to the rejection.

Her green eyes filled with tears and she blinked as she looked away.

I sat down beside him on the edge of the bed. "That isn't very nice, Grandpa. Ashling and I came here to see you, to spend some time with you. We didn't have to come, you know. Would you prefer we never visit, and you stay in this place all by yourself?"

Ashling flinched at my hard words and shot me a look that said it all, also known as *don't say the truth, Quinn, it hurts people.*

I shrugged. There was no point in pulling any punches. It wasn't likely he'd remember anyway and that made my guts twist up. I hated that he didn't know us, but I'd always felt like I could take it.

Ashling was the one it hurt the most. The one that took every word to heart and then some.

She sat on the other side of Grandpa, and forcibly took his hands in hers, speaking softly to him. I looked out the window, not really seeing the view, just thinking about how we'd come to this point in our trajectory.

Our family was a weird one at best. Growing up, Mom had all but ignored us, so busy as she was with her men and her girlfriends. Flitting around the globe whenever she could and leaving us with Grandpa for weeks, sometimes months, at a time. Though, if there was one of us she preferred, I suppose it would have been me—though saying she was kinder or loved me was a stretch. All it meant was that she hadn't completely ignored me. Even as a young child, at maybe four or five years old, I'd seen how her behavior toward us affected Ashling.

I'd seen how Ashling had reached for her, cried for her, and Mom just brushed her off. I tried to make up for it in my sister's life, tried to fill in the gap with all the things I could. Spending time with her, soothing her at night when a nightmare claimed her, doing what I could.

Grandpa, he'd favored Ashling in his own way,

coddling and spoiling her to the point where I wanted to pull my hair out while he taught me other things. He'd never treated me like a grandchild he'd loved, more like someone he was apprenticing. And then when things started to get bad, before we knew what was wrong with him, he'd spend days, even weeks acting as if I didn't exist. So really, it didn't surprise me that I'd always felt as if Ashling and I didn't fit, as if there was some gaping piece in our genetics that kept our mother from loving us.

That kept our family from being . . .normal.

Grandpa gave a sudden sharp grunt, silencing Ashling, then slowly turned to face me. His eyes were just like mine, a golden amber that had gained me more than my share of double takes growing up. If I never heard 'do you have contacts in?' again it would be too soon.

"You." He snarled, his face twisting up. "You will kill her. You damn filthy bitch," His hands flexed against his chest, the linen of his pale-yellow pajama top rippling under his fingers.

Ashling gasped and my eyes popped open wide that not only had he spoken directly to me, but that he'd cussed at me. "Grandpa watch your language," I said, my response automatic. It's what

Mom would say if she were here. She hated cursing, though it didn't bother me in the least.

He stood, fast, faster than I'd ever seen him move since he'd come into this place. I found myself scrambling back off the bed, for the first time uncertain about my own grandfather.

Ashling tugged on his sleeve. "Grandpa sit down. You're being silly."

He took a step, shook his head and the words exploded out of him. "YOU WILL KILL HER; YOU DAMN FILTHY BITCH!" His six-foot height towered over me and again I took a step back.

Never in my wildest dreams would I have thought he'd threaten either of us.

Ashling started to cry and I made a motion with my hand, a hang loose signal. It was our sign to get help when Grandpa was acting strange. I told myself I wasn't afraid—that this wasn't common, but it wasn't unheard of with him either. Lies, I told myself lies.

His barrel chest lifted and fell rapidly and those eyes so like my own narrowed on me.

I took another step back and lifted my hands into the air. "Okay then, Blake, I'll go." I started to sidle around him. At the last minute, I realized I should have just gone over the bed to avoid him, but then I'd never had him raise a hand to me before. Yelled at me, yes. Hit me? Never.

He lunged at me with that speed that I'd have not said was possible before that moment, his fingers wrapping around my throat before I could react. Shocked, I stared at him for a full second before I realized the trouble I was in, before I realized his hands were as strong as ever.

Ashling started to scream. "Somebody, help! He'll kill her!"

"That be the idea, Ashling, before she does you in like the filthy beast she is," he growled, his eyes fierce as they bored into mine. I fought his hands, clawing and scraping at the wrinkled skin, astounded at the strength in his old muscles. Like a fish dangling on a line, he lifted me up until the tips of my toes were all that touched the floor.

My body began to sag as the blood slowed to my brain, as my heart beat faster in an attempt to make something happen. Distantly, I knew what was happening, that I was dying, but I couldn't stop it. The black dots that danced in front of my eyes were bigger with each passing second, spreading and filling my vision as my heart and blood slowed in tandem.

Voices, footsteps, more yelling. Someone was

screaming, someone was crying. Not how the day was supposed to go, I was sure of it. Through it all, those hands stayed locked around my neck. His fingernails drew blood, the warmth trickling down my back.

In the fog of my brain a voice whispered. It sounded like my grandpa, but younger. It sounded like my Grandpa who'd given me advice for so many years. Advice I'd tucked away and believed with all my heart.

It be better this way, Quinn. You must be believing me that to be quickened by me is better than the others that would draw forth your powers. Protect your sister, above all else. She needs your love and the safety you will bring.

I wanted to ask why he was trying to kill me if he'd wanted me to take care of Ashling. What had I done to make this happen, to make him hate me so? Tears burned at the edges of my eyes.

All my life I'd wanted him to love me, too, as he loved Ashling, not just as someone to teach, but someone to truly love. His voice was as clear as if we stood across from one another, as clear as if he were not trying to strangle me to death.

I loved you both, but she needed me more, and you needed to be strong. She will need you now that I'm gone. I have used ta last of what makes me whole to quicken your blood, granddaughter. I am no more.

And with that, the darkness that threatened at the edge of my mind swallowed me whole, and everything that I knew vanished.

2

Almost dying was not the way to start the day, but apparently that was my lot in life. I was alive, I knew that much, and we were with Grandpa in his room when he'd attacked me. When he'd tried to strangle the life out of me.

Protect your sister, above all else. She needs your love and the safety you will bring.

Grandpa's voice seemed to echo through me, sharpening all my senses.

"Quinn, wake up!" Hands shook me, and I gasped as I opened my eyes, sitting up reflexively even though it tugged and pulled on all the muscles of my body. Or seemed to anyway.

"No, let her lie still for a minute. We are so

sorry, Ms. Lorcan. We had no idea your grandfather had it in him to attack someone. Especially one of you girls. He talks about you all the time," one of the male attendants said. I couldn't remember his name right then. To be honest I was just glad I was waking up at all. The moment the darkness had swallowed me whole I'd more than thought I'd be staring at a bright light as I died fully.

I didn't think I'd be staring up at the bright fluorescent lights of the Eric Martin Pavilion.

The two attendants laid me back on the cool linoleum floor. I rubbed my neck carefully, wincing. What felt like crescent shaped cuts from his fingernails still oozed here and there and I knew from the tenderness that I was going to be badly bruised.

I tried sitting up again, and this time the world didn't spin.

"Quinn!" Ashling threw herself at me the way she'd thrown herself at Grandpa just a short time ago. I caught her with one hand, using the other to brace myself.

"I'm okay, Ash," I whispered into her hair, the scratch of my vocal cords against my throat painful.

"I'm so sorry. It was my idea to come and see him before we go out to Tofino," she said.

I let out a hoarse attempt of a laugh, my throat aching with each noise I made.

"S'okay." I patted her back. "Not your fault."

"I'm sorry," she said again, green eyes full of tears that trickled down her cheeks. I sat up a little better, and wiped her tears away, the motion a reflex that I'd honed over our life taking care of one another.

"Don't cry. Nobody got hurt, right?" I asked. The attendants around us lifted eyebrows. Okay, so I had gotten hurt, but that didn't count.

"We sent Blake off to the infirmary while you were coming around to check his blood pressure," the same male attendant said.

I shared a look with Ashling. We both knew it was more likely he was being sent for some hard-core sedatives and some sort of evaluation that would land him deeper in the facility, maybe the second or third floor down.

"We don't have to go to Tofino," Ashling said. "We can reschedule and go another time." She wiped her face, smearing mascara which only made her look younger.

I really, really, didn't want to go to Tofino and she knew it. Maybe I could use it as an out?

They helped me stand, and then the attendants escorted us through the pavilion—right out the front doors. They suggested I go to the hospital next door. I declined. I hated hospitals and as long as I was standing, able to breathe, see, and hear, I wasn't going into one voluntarily. It was bad enough going to the institute even for Grandpa.

I rubbed at my face.

"Tofino?" She asked softly.

I managed to keep the groan inside of me and even managed a weak smile. "We'll go. I know how important it is to you."

Ashling held out her hands in a gimme motion, and I reluctantly let her take the keys from me. "I'm driving. Who knows what brain damage you have now?" she crinkled up her face at me.

"Sympathy, thy name is not sister." I mumbled.

"Look, you're the one who said you're okay." She pointed out, and she was right, I had said that. Didn't mean I was actually right.

She unlocked the car and I let myself into the passenger side, slumping into the seat.

"You want to go to the hospital?" She asked, her voice softening once more.

I shook my head, and instantly regretted it. Shooting pains through my neck and shoulders had me leaning against the passenger door. Ashling didn't see me. I pulled myself together before she looked over at me.

"No, I'm fine. He's old and I think I just passed out. Nothing major." I said with my eyes closed and choosing not to acknowledge the pain up and down my neck or the throbbing in my skull.

She was quiet long enough that I knew she was trying to figure out how to broach the subject of Grandpa and the attempted murder scene.

"What do you think happened? To make him try to hurt you?" Ashling finally asked as she turned onto Highway 19, heading north at a speed that would get her in trouble if any cop saw us.

Leaning back in the seat, I kept my eyes closed so I wouldn't have to see her weave in and out of traffic as was her wont. I could feel it, which was enough to add a turned stomach to the throbbing headache. None of which would be helped when we hit the far side of the highway that led across the island. That section was built on 'S' curves that rolled up and down like a damn rollercoaster.

"I really don't know," I said, "I mean, who was I supposed to kill do you think?"

Ashling was quiet for another long stretch. I finally opened one eye and peeked at her. Face tight with worry, she chewed heavily on her bottom lip as her fingers clenched and flexed on the steering wheel. Not a good sign when it came to my little sister.

"Ash? Talk to me."

She shrugged and switched lanes without signaling, a series of honks going up around us. I cringed and closed my eyes again as flecks of dark spots trickled through my vision.

I didn't want to start a fight and with her it was quite possible that just by pushing her into answering me, it would happen. And then the headache would only escalate.

She cleared her throat. "I don't know. But I know this is going to sound crazy so please don't lock me up like Grandpa but . . .I thought I heard something inside my head while he was strangling you. Like words."

My eyes popped open; headache still there but momentarily forgotten as I sat up. "Pull over."

She didn't argue, just pulled to the side of the road as soon as there was a place to do so. We were near Goldstream, a massive park off the highway with trees that towered over the pathways which wound along the river. The water ran parallel to the highway, though the cars that zipped by us shook the Explorer, it was all overpowered by the sound of the water.

"You heard something too? Because I heard a voice when he was strangling me," I said, my hand going to my throat. She turned to me; her eyes wide as saucers.

"It sounded like Grandpa . . ." She said then covered her face with her hands. "But how could he have been in my head talking when he wasn't saying anything?"

"He spoke to me too," I said, "And he sounded like he did before he went into the facility." She nodded and I tried to swallow, wincing at the pain.

Ashling spun sideways in her seat to face me, the straps of her bright red bikini showing underneath her tank top. "He said to me that we needed each other. That no matter what, I was to stick close to you. Not to let anyone between us. To not doubt the bond between us no matter what."

Chills swept through me and I found myself worrying at my bottom lip too for a moment—a bad trait we both had. I forced myself to stop. Rubbing my hands on my bare thighs, the jean shorts and T-shirt I wore suddenly seemed like not enough clothes as the air conditioning felt like ice against my skin.

"What did he say to you?" she asked, her voice barely above a whisper, the tremor in her words saying it all. This felt crazy. And in our family, crazy was a definite and real fear.

Again, I swallowed and wanted to curse at myself for doing it. I dug around in the back seat of the vehicle and found a bottle of water, took a sip with a grimace and then spoke. "He said that I was to look after you now that he was gone. And something about quickening my blood." I waved my hand in the air. "It didn't really make sense, other than to look after you. But why would that change now? We've always looked out for each other. We've always had each other's backs."

Ashling stared out at the forest and the people walking under the tall trees pointing out sights in the park, taking pictures, happy in their sightseeing. Outside of the car felt like a different world suddenly. "I don't know. I mean, if it was just me hearing voices, I'd say maybe I was like Grandpa, but you heard him too." Her eyes closed and she let out a slow, unsteady breath. "You know when the storms come in off the straight? How the air changes and the smell of the wind even shifts? We all know what's coming, but we can't see the storm yet?"

Her words were not helping the chills running through my body. She opened her eyes. "It feels like that, right now. Like there's a storm on the horizon that we can't see, but we are already feeling the pressure pushing down on us." Her eyes stared off into the distance and I wondered what she was seeing. A storm in the literal sense, or something else?

Because everything she was saying was exactly how I felt. Only to me it was like the coming of the night, not a storm. Like that split second while the sun hung onto the sky and you'd think that the sunset was going to last forever, and then blink . . .it was gone and you stood in the twilight hour, all the colors of the world muted.

I reached over, and put a hand on her arm, my fingertips brushing against the gooseflesh that had risen all over her skin and seeing the same reaction on my own forearms.

"Maybe we shouldn't go to Tofino," I said. "Maybe we should stay home. What if this is some sort of weird premonition?" I cringed a little on that last word, our mother would have laughed at us for believing in the otherworldly.

Her shoulders slumped. Ah, damn it all. I didn't want this day that was supposed to be a celebration, to be added to the list of disappointments in her life. She'd had enough of those already with the way our family was, never mind Grandpa's freak out.

This was supposed to be her graduation present from me, a trip to Tofino. Mom hadn't even bothered to give Ash a card for her graduation before jetting off to Ireland chasing some new man or some such. She'd said no more than two words after she'd left.

Staring out the windshield at the passing traffic I thought about what going to Tofino meant. For me, it was going into the surf again, facing the fears that wanted to swallow me whole even here, this far from the ocean. I broke out into another cold sweat at the thought of going into the water.

But this wasn't about me, this was about Ashling and making sure she had at least some good memories. Pulling on my tattered big girl panties that had surely taken a beating already for the day, I took one more swig of water and spoke slowly.

"You know what? Never mind, we aren't going to let Grandpa and some crazy voices inside our heads stop us. This is, after all, your graduation gift. And if we're both going crazy, we can get a double room at the Pavilion when we get back." I squeezed her arm and she looked up, a small smile on her lips. I answered it with a grin and a wink.

"Really?" Her shoulders came up high, almost to her ears.

I grinned and nodded my head very carefully. "Here's the deal. We won't talk about the craziness that is our family or what happened with Grandpa today, or any weird feelings we are getting. We'll go and have fun; we'll eat great food and enjoy a well-deserved weekend and then we can deal with whatever this all is after we get home. Okay?"

She smiled, wariness still in her eyes but we'd essentially called a truce. Not between each other, but between us and the scary shit. That would be good enough for now. I leaned back in my seat, rubbing my arms, trying to get my own gooseflesh to calm down. "Now, onward, chauffeur," I said, pointing to the highway. "We cannot be late for our appointment with destiny."

Why I used that word, I wish I knew, for it turned out to be all too apropos.

Ashling let out a laugh, threw the car into gear and hit the gas. The far too worn tires of my '99

Explorer not only squealed on the pavement but also spit loose gravel out behind us with a spray that caused more than a few horns to honk at us once more.

I clamped my eyes shut. Ash swerved us out into traffic with the vigor of a NASCAR driver. My stomach rolled and my head throbbed.

This was going to be a very, very long drive.

3

We stopped only once on the drive at Cathedral Grove, a forest of trees that were the oldest and biggest on Vancouver Island. Made up of western red cedars, they were the same variety as those that grew in the redwoods in California. Not that I'd ever been there, but I hoped to go one day.

I stood and stretched my legs as Ashling grabbed her cell phone and ran deeper into the forest to do some nature selfies. "I'll be back!" She yelped over her shoulder.

How could four years between us feel like so many more? There was nothing in me that wanted to go prancing through a forest and snag snapshots. A grimace slid over my lips as I made my way slower into the forest. The sound of birds and wildlife was soothing, washing away a little of the shock and trauma from the morning's adventure.

I found a downed log and sat down, Ash in the distance as she leaned against a tree and pouted her lips. "You look like a duck!" I hollered, breaking the pristine sounds of the forest.

She flipped me a finger and we both laughed.

This place wasn't one we got to often, but I always liked the feel of it. A bit like coming home in a way, to a place that was always calm.

A shuffle in the leaves on the ground, to my left turned my head. I winced at the minor twinge of pain but then my eyes widened rapidly. Not because of the pain either.

The diamond shaped, bright red head of a rather large snake lifted and let out a long low hiss.

Body running on survivor autopilot I scrambled back as the snake settled back under the leave. "Ash, time to go!" I yelled as I booked it back to the path. She jogged toward me.

"What?"

"Snake." I said. I wasn't afraid of them, but that was no native to our area snake. I didn't know what kind, but I knew when people had let their exotic pets loose. "Someone got tired of their venomous snake and let it go."

She squeaked and ran down the path toward the car and I was quick to follow.

Back in the car we called the local wildlife conservation and they said they'd check it out.

I leaned in my seat. "You still good to drive?" The headache that had been fading made a full resurgence with the burst of adrenaline.

"Yeah, let's get out of here, the sooner we get to Tofino the better." She said as she threw the car in drive and booted it down the highway once more. Much as I hated how she drove, I had to agree. The sooner we got this trip truly over with, the better.

"THIS ROOM IS AMAZING, QUINN! LOOK AT THE view, I can practically see Japan!" Ashling squealed. She dropped her bags, and then inspected the corner room I'd rented for the three nights we were here in Tofino. Seven hundred and fifty bucks a night, and it wasn't even the best room they had, but the smile on her face was worth every hour of overtime I'd put in to make it happen.

The Wickaninnish Inn was the best hotel on

the west coast of Vancouver Island, and my wallet could attest to that even if the reviews on the place had not. I'd saved up money every month for the last year in preparation for Ashling's graduation gift. I'd known even a year ago that Mom wouldn't do anything, though I had tried to persuade her before she left for Ireland.

That hadn't gone well.

"Come on, Mom, at least a card, maybe a gift certificate. Money stuffed in an envelope, hell, anything at this point! She's your daughter and this is a big day for her!" Anger had fueled my words. How she could be so callous to her own daughter was beyond me. I knew from experience that Ashling would get nothing for her graduation, but I had to try. For her sake I would swallow my pride and beg.

Mom—or Darcy, as she demanded Ashling call her—had just shrugged and looked away. But in a quick flash I could see the shame in her eyes, the guilt. What I didn't understand was why she kept on acting like she did if she felt bad. "I have to go, Quinn. Look after your sister. Try to keep her out of trouble."

"I always have, Darcy. Because unlike you, I love her."

The sad thing was that I don't think she'd even realized that the part about her not loving her own daughter had been what had upset her. I'd never called her Darcy before, and her whole body had stiffened as I used her name, as if an iron rod had been shoved down her spine.

I'd driven her to the airport in silence after that and hadn't even hugged her goodbye, just pulled over at the international departures and let her get her own luggage out. Maybe the time in Ireland would do her some good, give her some perspective on how she had handled raising her two girls. I doubted it, but hoped for it, nonetheless. No matter how many times she ran away, she always came back the same.

An exclamation from Ashling brought me back to the present. She had just found the private bar and was currently holding up several tiny bottles with a wide grin on her face. "I'm like a giant!"

I rolled my eyes, "Tiny bottles that cost twice what a regular size bottle does."

I made my way into the bathroom and flicked on the light. The image in the mirror that stared back at me was unexpected to say the least.

My neck was black and purple with red crescent moons where Grandpa's fingers had sliced me. The soreness had faded on the ride across the island, and while I hadn't exactly forgotten about the attack, with the fading of the pain the rest had seemed distant. The mirror countered those thoughts strongly.

"Well, that is just gorgeous," I muttered.

Ashling joined me in the bathroom as I turned away from the mirror. The tub was easily big enough for two people with swooping sides and fresh soaps laid out along the edge. The floor tile in the room was a beautiful white with flecks and veins of gold running through it that made me think it could have been marble.

Ashling hugged me. "You're the best sister, you know that right?"

"Don't have to tell me that," I said, and hugged her back, glad I'd spent the extra money for the nice room. "You remember that the next time you throw a fit about me eating the last cookie."

She laughed and went back to the main room where a king-sized bed took up a large portion of the space, the duvet thick and inviting.

Much as I wanted to lay down and close my eyes, I went to the window and stared out at the beach below us. Chesterman Beach was known for its waves and surfing even though the waters were cool. But that's why we were here—the surfing, not the cool water. Ashling wanted to learn how to surf. She hoped to go to Hawaii next year with some girlfriends and wanted to know how to ride the waves before she played tourist.

Sweat trickled down my back despite the air conditioning. I'd never told Ashling how badly I was afraid of the water after my accident down in Mexico. Didn't think I needed to, and I wasn't about to admit my fear to her now.

"Dum, dum." She hummed as low as she could. "Dum, dum." My back stiffened, and my gut clenched as she kept on going. "Dum, dum, dum, dum, dum, dum."

The Jaws theme did not impress me. I turned only my head to her, impressed at how much better my neck was feeling despite the terrible bruising.

"Not funny, Ashling. Next time you get dragged around by a shark, let's see how you like watching Jaws," I walked away from the window doing what I could to not let her see the fear.

"Oh, lighten up, Quinn. You've got a little wee scar, and you haven't gone in the water since Mexico, which was like a year ago. This will be good for you," she said, unpacking her bag, and hanging her clothes up.

I disagreed with her, but I was doing this for

her which meant that I was going to do it, no matter how much it freaked me out. I slid my flip flops back on and went to the door.

"I'm going to go find out about a surfing instructor, preferably one that will let you drown," I said.

She laughed as I stepped out of the room and shut the door behind me. She would think I was playing, not really angry, and she would be right. I wasn't angry, but it was a good cover for the fear that had spiked through me. I really didn't want to go into the water.

Sure, there were no sharks per-se in the cool waters off the west coast of the island, at least nothing to be worried about. But my body and PTSD didn't know that. Water was water.

I made my way down to the hotel lobby where the concierge gave me a few numbers to try. I stepped outside to call the different surfing schools. After dialing through to five and leaving messages, I finally spoke to a real person on the sixth call.

"Hi, I'm looking for someone to take my sister —and me, I guess—surfing over the next couple of days. Do you have anyone available?" I asked.

The speaker's voice was smooth and rich, like

liquid chocolate and I found myself leaning against the banister that wrapped around the inn, lightheaded. A reminder that I'd been almost strangled, I was sure.

"Yes," He said slowly, the words a drawl I couldn't quite place, "I could come and teach the two of you to surf without a problem. I had a cancellation and could meet you early tomorrow morning if you like. First lesson's free."

That perked me up. My budget wasn't exactly enormous, and a free lesson was all I needed to seal the deal. "Really? That would be awesome. Thanks. We're staying at the Wickaninnish. Can you meet us at Chesterman Beach?"

"Sure. I'll see you two at six a.m., just after sunrise." His voice grew faint and I could tell he was about to hang up.

"Wait, how will we recognize you?"

"Don't worry, Quinn. I'll find you." The click of the call ending made me frown. Something was off about that whole conversation.

I trotted up the stairs to our room and had to knock on the door. I'd left my key card inside in the hurry to get away from my sister and her teasing. Ashling didn't come to the door right away, though I could hear her moving around inside.

Probably spreading out her way-too-many bags of stuff she'd brought.

It was as I waited for Ashling to open the door that I realized the instructor had called me by my name—but I'd never given it to him. A wave of unease rippled through me. I tried to shake it off, but the feeling wouldn't leave me.

How the hell could he have known my name?

"Ashling, open the damn door!" I yelled, my uncertainty about the phone call disappearing under my sudden irritation.

I heard a giggle, and then the door creeped open with the chain still on, and a pair of green eyes peering out at me. "Yes, can I help you?"

I let out an exasperated sigh. "Let me in or I will cancel our appointment for surfing lessons tomorrow."

She let out a screech that raised the hairs on the back of my neck and opened the door. I stepped in and shut it firmly behind me.

The rest of the evening went smoothly. Dinner was fantastic, the best food I'd ever eaten, all done with local foods and with a skill that I envied. We splurged on several desserts, which we took up to our room and ate throughout the night. Finally, around two a.m., Ashling tumbled into bed. She fell asleep within seconds. It was a gift she had if you discounted the light snoring.

I tidied up the room, put our dirty plates outside the door for housekeeping and set the alarm for five a.m. I let out a soft groan. Three hours wasn't enough sleep. I wasn't a teenager like Ashling anymore with unlimited energy and no cares in the world. At the ripe old age of twenty-two, I felt ancient next to my eighteen-year-old sister.

I crawled into bed beside her, and like when she had a bad dream as a little girl, I curled up around her, holding her tightly. Within moments, I had fallen asleep, too, and although I knew that, the dream that took me over still caught me off guard.

I stood in Cathedral Grove, the oldest living forest on Vancouver Island. Next to me was the downed log that I'd sat on, and I found myself turning to the left. There was the snake with unusual brilliant blue scales and a head that looked as though it had been dipped in red paint. The same damn snake I'd seen when we'd stopped in the grove earlier.

And she—yes, *she*—was talking. Only it wasn't like her mouth flapped or moved. Her words came as thought inside my head, loud and clear as her solidly black eyes locked on my own.

"You will be reborn, Quinn." Her voice echoed through my head, and a deep chanting rose around us as though a multitude of people were with us, though I saw no one else. Pain erupted throughout my body in every pore, coming from nowhere that I could see, and pulsing in time with the beat of the chanting. It was as if the very earth and trees picked up on the rhythm of pain that rippled through me as the branches and world leaned in closer, surrounding me.

Each strange word spoken caused my blood to pulse and filled me with an agony I couldn't escape. I stumbled to the side, catching myself on the downed log as animal noises escaped my mouth unbidden.

The pressure points where Grandpa's hands and fingers had bit into me filled with an intense heat that increased, multiplying exponentially the longer the dream went on. At one point I fell to the ground and wrapped my own hands around my neck as if I could stop the burning that coursed through me. As if I could pull it all away from me and stop the pain, as if I could put out the flames that didn't exist but that I could feel charring my skin.

A scream curled out of me shattering the chants for a brief second, but even that didn't slow the fire.

"You will become what your destiny calls you to become." The snake's voice said.

A new pain started low in my belly, not fire like the ring of pain around my neck, but sharp slices deep in my guts as if I was being skewered on a razor-sharp knife. Over and over, the phantom blade ripped into me until the screams once more ripped through me. A large hand clamped over my lips, rough with callouses and I tasted the spray of the ocean on the palm that kept my screams inside of me.

There were no thoughts running through me by that point, just the desire to stop whatever it was that was slicing through me over and over. My jaw flexed and I bit down on the palm over my mouth, blood coating my tongue in an instant. Not a coppery tang of pennies, but something more akin to wine. Rich, decadent, vibrant with life and light there was a sense of the person holding me down, a man I thought, in the stupor of pain that held me tight. But that was all I could put together.

"You will be a warrior," the snake said.

The chanting around us picked up speed, echoing the rapid fearful beating of my heart and the rush of blood through my veins. Sweat poured down the sides of my face as I huddled on the ground, curled tight around myself.

The man that had been holding me was still there though I didn't see him. My eyes were closed, his hands held tight to mine, one slick with blood where I'd bitten him. I tried to open my eyes, blinked a little but could see nothing past the haze of pain and fire that filled my vision.

"Hang on, Quinn, it's almost over." A voice finally that was not the snake. One that I recognized but in the fog of everything I couldn't place where he was from. Only that it was soothing, and I hung onto the sounds of his voice for all I was worth. A hand brushed a stray curl from my forehead. "Almost done."

"You will be a leader." The snake's voice rippled through me.

The screams began again, ripping out of me without warning. They were shrill, shrieking screams, that of a dying and wounded animal that hadn't yet given up and the horror that came with them was that I couldn't believe I could even make those sounds. But even they faded into moans as my voice and lungs gave out, as I was sure I was dying. No one could survive this kind of pain and I finally gave myself over to that reality.

"You will save your world and ours." She whispered.

Tears streamed down my face as the chanting around us slowed, the crippling, mind numbing pain receding into nothing but a dull ache that spread through my limbs and torso. I lay on the ground, a hand stroking my hair until that faded into something far rougher.

Something I wanted to ignore as the dream broke apart, shattering my sleep.

Hands shook me hard enough to thump my head into the pillow. Ashling leaned over me, tears streaming down her face, matching mine as I fully came to. The morning light had barely started to filter in through the window. Our alarm hadn't yet gone off.

The pain from my dream was distant, though I remembered it as if it had really happened.

"What happened?" I croaked out. "Was I talking in my sleep?"

"You were screaming. I couldn't get you to wake up," she hiccupped back a sob.

This trip seemed doomed to be a disaster from the beginning. I reached out and put a hand on her shoulder and tugged her toward me. She fell against me, body shuddering. "That was the worst sound I've ever heard in my life," she said, her words muffled against my shoulder. "It was like you were being pulled apart. It was like you were dying!"

Her words sent waves of remembered pain through me. I bit my lower lip to keep from whimpering, the memory of the nightmare fading already.

"I think I'm going to get up now. Bad dreams, that's all it was. Just bad dreams." I said.

The alarm went off making us both jump. I slammed a hand down on it. "Don't need that."

I stood and wobbled my way to the bathroom, my unruly blond curls covering half my face as I stared in the mirror. I stared hard before a gasp escaped my lips. Ashling ran over to me, worry etched into her face. "What is it?"

I lifted a hand to my neck where just a few short hours ago I had been battered and bruised, swollen and sore. Now the skin was smooth and unblemished as if it had never happened.

Ashling brushed the hair off the back of my

neck. “The bruises are all gone back here too,” she whispered. I took a deep breath, held it and then slowly let it out. I swallowed and there wasn’t even a whisper of pain.

Nope, I was not going to freak out. I managed a smile, forcing it across my lips. “Lucky I heal quick, I guess.”

I turned and hurried back to my luggage, feeling Ashling’s eyes boring into my back.

“Yeah,” she said, “I guess. But you’ve never had anything heal that fast—”

I cut her off. “No, no buts. Today is going to be a good day, okay?” I kept that forced smile on my lips. “No more nightmares, no more weirdness, only an awesome day.”

She nodded slowly, but even I could see that she didn’t believe me anymore than I believed me.

If only we’d known just what the day would bring, a nightmare and some fast healing bruises would have been the least of our concerns.

4

The cool, wet sand slid through my toes as I scrunched them up at the edge of the water. The Pacific Ocean lay out ahead of me, full of all sorts of things which were not limited to things with teeth, tentacles, and a variety of creatures that would for no good reason, eat me.

All of which brought back the sensations of the dream from only a few hours before. I swallowed hard and tried to push that away. This was not the place.

This was a day for Ashling.

A rolling wave splashed around my ankles, sliding across my skin, a lover's caress. I stepped back, away from the invitation. The wetsuit I was wearing only came to mid-calf and was hardly a protection against the cold water of the Pacific. Chesterman Beach was beautiful, everything the package had promoted it to be and then some. I hoped that Ashling appreciated what it took for me to be here—to face my fears for her. She didn't seem any worse for the wear after our short—and my nightmare-filled—night. I, on the other hand, found myself stifling yawns and daydreaming of sleeping the afternoon away.

I fingered the sheath on my upper thigh which held the knife Grandpa had given me right before he went into the institution. I'd wondered at the gift at the time. Gifts weren't really his forte, and everything he'd given me up until then had been advice, and training.

But when I'd told him that I was going diving in Mexico he'd been insistent that I have this old knife of his.

"Where do you be going?" Grandpa asked, his amber eyes sweeping up from where he'd been reading his newspaper.

"Mexico," I said. "With Myranda and JoJo. We're going to go diving, they found some cheap courses

down there we can take and then go dive in open water." I paused in washing his dishes, up to my elbows in suds as per his request so as to make sure I, and I quote, 'used enough damn soap to drown the buggers on my plates'.

"When are you going?" He stood and folded his paper, laying it on his seat.

"Next month," I rinsed off another plate, again wishing that Grandpa would break down and buy a damn dishwasher.

He walked out of the kitchen where he'd been over-seeing me. A moment later I could hear him shuffling around in his bedroom, the sound of something being dragged across the old wooden floors and the click of a latch.

"Quinn, can you come here?" He called out, surprising me. Taking me away from an unfinished task was a big deal.

I dried my hands on a ratty old tea towel and headed toward his bedroom. I stood in the doorway; hands still damp. Grandpa sat on the edge of his bed, his big hands holding something tight enough that I could only see a bit of leather on each end, nothing else.

"You need to take this with you," he opened his hands and held out a knife in a sheath.

I blinked a few times. "What do I need a knife for?

Grandpa, I'm going diving. In Mexico. Not slashing through the Amazon jungle or anything." I laughed, but he didn't.

"Here, here. Take it," he pushed it into my hands. The knife had a bone handle, its blade about eight inches long with intricate engravings swirling down the back of the razor-sharp edge.

"Always take it with you when you go in the water. Promise me. That's when the monsters come," Grandpa said. "They come from the deep and they will have you if they can."

OF COURSE, I'D TAKEN THE KNIFE AND GIVEN HIM MY promise that I would keep it with me. For the last year where his sanity had held, it had been the same fears. The monsters he saw waiting in the dark of the forest around his house, in the water, in the night, he feared they would come for the rest of us. So even if I wasn't the granddaughter he'd treated with great care, it was better according to him that I survive, and the monsters die. That's why he'd been teaching me.

I shook my head, scattering the thoughts.

I hated to admit it, but I took comfort in the

knife and did indeed take it with me diving when I went to Mexico.

Maybe the monster hadn't been the one he'd seen coming, but something had come from the depths that much was true. And the knife had saved me.

I gritted my teeth as memories rushed through my mind and threatened to suck me into a panic attack.

Me and my two friends had been out on the boat, open water all around us, the heat of the Mexican sun beating down on us. Dressed in bikinis and light weight scuba gear we fell into the water with great glee.

The area we were in was well known for scuba diving, what we didn't know was that a few boats had been chumming the area the day before.

We swam down, under the waves into the beautiful clear water.

Everything that came next happened so fast it was a blur.

A sharp pain in my left calf, like a thousand tiny needles and at the same time a pressure against my bone that felt as if it would snap.

I turned my head, saw the wide nose of the

shark, the black eye that was looking past me. My friends had fled, leaving me there under the water with the shark that for whatever reason was for lack of a better word, holding me. I grabbed my knife that I'd worn on a nylon sheath across my hips, my Grandpa's knife. With a swift jab, I drove the tip into the shark's nose, and it spit me out, swimming away as I floundered there in the blue water.

Bright blue water.

Brighter red blood.

Swimming to the top with one leg, sure I was about to be grabbed from below again.

Using slow even breaths, I managed to get my heart rate to a normal level as the scene from Mexico spooled out through me. Okay, almost normal as I shuddered and sucked for air as if I were being pulled back into the boat again.

The screaming of my friends.

The captain telling me I was lucky, just a juvenile bull shark by the look of it.

I shook my head, trying to clear it. Those memories needed to stay in the past where they belonged. Especially today.

Basically, while surfing out in the Pacific was what Ashling wanted, it was not my idea of a good time. Surfing on the west coast of Vancouver Island was even less of a good idea, at least to me though in theory I knew it meant there were fewer biting things.

The water was cold, even with the heat of the summer bearing down on us, and it was known for its riptides and jagged rocks as much as its surfing. So, a whole different set of things that could kill us.

And yet, here we were.

"Come on, Quinn, that water is great, and the waves are bitch'n!" Ashling yelled from a good hundred feet from the shore, maybe more. The water started off shallow and took a long time to hit a drop off.

I stared at her out in the water, sitting on her surfboard waiting for our instructor to join her, unruly strawberry blond curls escaping her pony-tail and dancing in the wind. She hadn't even put on the surfboard leash, cocky little thing that she was, prancing her way into the water.

I waved at her and forced a smile to my lips though she probably couldn't see my face well at that distance. I wouldn't ruin this day for her. This was her moment, her celebration.

I could do this for her.

"I hate this," I muttered under my breath.

"Then why are you here?" a strong male voice

asked me, rich in tones. It belonged to our instructor, Luke. Damn it if the voice I'd heard on the phone more than matched the guy it was attached to which made it hard to look at him.

You can't really call guys beautiful and not think feminine, but this one had nailed it down.

He was a damn beauty and I had a hard time looking at him. Drop dead gorgeous wouldn't even begin to describe him. Not too tall, maybe 5'10", with blond hair cut short except for the top bit which was longer, and he kept finger combing backward. The color seemed to shimmer in the sunlight, and he had the bluest eyes, like those Mexican waters I'd swum in, so bright that I couldn't look away once I locked eyes with him. Which meant I wasn't looking at him in the face so as to keep from being unable to look away. I swallowed hard and stared at the sand at my feet. He was far too pretty, far too dangerous, with his silky voice that made me forget my own name.

To say the least, Ashling had been delighted when she saw him and realized he was our surfing instructor. Flirting and prancing around in her little red bikini, she'd been obviously determined to get his attention. But while he was kind to her, he didn't fall into her arms as she'd been not so subtly hoping. Secretly, I was laughing, not in a mean way, more in a sisterly this never happens way. Because she was so pretty, petite, and feminine, she wasn't used to men turning her down.

Which is what had led her to leave us behind on the beach and go out into the water on her own.

I fingered the cuffs on my wetsuit, the anxiety starting to build again even as I tried to push it down.

"I promised her we could do anything she wanted for her graduation gift." I said, "So this is what we are doing."

We were the only ones on this part of the beach, the early morning was enough to scare many of the tourists away as well as the die-hard locals, by the looks of it. From what the brochure had said, usually the beach was flooded, despite the cooler water and the mist that wouldn't burn off till afternoon. I could see a few surfers riding the waves in the distance, black specks on the water.

Hardcore.

"You must care for her a great deal," Luke said. He sounded surprised. "To bring her here when you are afraid of the water."

I frowned at him not liking that he read me so

easily. “She’s my baby sister. Of course, I care about her. And I’m not afraid of the water. I’m afraid of what’s in it.”

“I’d hoped that wasn’t the case,” he said, his voice soft. My frown deepened and a trickle of alarm started at the base of my spine.

“What the hell is that supposed to mean? Why would you hope that I wouldn’t care about my sister? You think because you’re passably cute you can say crap like that?” Each word grew sharper in my mouth as I frowned at him. He didn’t have a chance to answer me.

“Quinn!” Ashling’s yell was sharp and far too high pitched. Not her usual light, airy tones, which meant she wasn’t playing. I spun to see her still out in the water, but off her board. She gripped the surfboard and her head was all of her that I could see.

This was no game.

I didn’t hesitate—though my body quailed with remembered fear and pain, I didn’t think about anything except getting her out of the water and getting to her. I was not my friends; I wouldn’t leave her out there.

I took one step and arms encircled me, holding me tight and stopping me from diving into the surf. "She'll be fine. Let her be." Luke said. "Let her go."

Let her go? What in hell was he talking about?

"Damn it, let *me* go!" I yelled, jerking my body left and right in a vain attempt to free myself. Luke's grip only tightened as he held me away from the water, dragging me back. His arms were like vises around my middle, unmovable. I twisted again, using a move Grandpa had taught me to slide down and out of a hold.

Luke grunted as I came up with a knee. He barely blocked me from hitting his family jewels, pushing my blow to hit his inner thigh instead. He still had me by one hand though, and his fingers were tight around my wrist.

"Quinn!" Ashling's voice went up another octave and I twisted in time to see her head bob down on the last bit of my name, her voice turning into a gurgle. Something large and black, skin shiny with slime, breached in the water next to her then slid back under the waves, the hump easily three feet out of the water. My heart constricted with horror, and my body thundered with adrenaline. It had to be a killer whale, even though I didn't see a fin. That was the only thing out here that *big* that could be attacking her. We didn't have sharks that size on the west coast. At least, not that I knew of. God, I hoped not. I couldn't face that again.

Luke held my wrist with a strength that said it all. He was not letting me go. It made no sense though, what did he care if I went into the water after her?

"Quinn, please believe me, you can't go in the water." His voice caressed my skin, and his words reverberating inside my skull until I believed them. I relaxed and he pulled me into his arms with my back to his chest. A wave of fatigue swept over me as my head leaned back. I slumped as my blood slowed and the fear left me.

A small part of my mind said that this was wrong, that I had to fight him. That he was doing something to me. The other part told that first part to shut up.

Luke was right. I couldn't go in the water. Ashling would be okay. She was a strong swimmer and this, his arms around me, felt so nice. Maybe she was just playing with me again. Like humming the theme to *Jaws*. He turned me to face him, putting my back to the ocean and the distant cries of the gulls and the water faded. His hand came up and stroked my face. He brushed an errant curl back and tucked it behind my ear.

"Ah, Quinn, you've got to let her go. It will be easier this way, to say goodbye now rather than later. I know that's hard to hear, but you must trust me that I know what's best for you." He leaned down, holding my face in his hands as his thumbs rubbed intricate designs on my cheeks. His lips pressed into mine. Kissing me? Why would he do that, I didn't even know him?

His lips were warm, and a burst of that warmth curled through my veins, as if I were kissing the sunlight itself, golden and safe. The touch and heat woke parts of me I had no idea were even there, stirring some long dormant piece inside of me, something that I suddenly knew Grandpa's attack had awakened in me.

The empty pieces that had left me hollow my whole life filled my body, sealing the broken bits together.

Quickened.

Pushing up against Luke's energy, was something that felt . . .like my own . . .power? I wasn't sure that was the right word.

Whatever strength it was that rose inside of me, it was my own and it rippled through me. My nerve endings flashing as though lightning danced through me, burning off the fog of his touch and mouth, clearing my mind. Tingling from head to toe, I pulled away striving to untangle my limbs from his. Though I didn't understand it, I felt the power and knew it for what it was though it seemed as crazy as Grandpa.

Magic.

Magic that gave me the strength to fight what Luke was trying to do to me. It burned through me, a cleansing fire that undid the power he wrapped around me to bend me to his will.

"Ashling," I gasped out. Luke pulled back, a frown slipping over his beautiful face, marring it, taking the glamor away.

I slid my hand down my thigh to the knife sheath. "Let me go!" I said, again trying to pull myself out of his arms to no avail.

"Trust me, Quinn. I'm saving your life right now. If you go into that water, you'll not come back out. You have to trust me," he said, the power in his voice making an attempt to sweep over me again. Like a hypnotist. I bit down on the inside of my cheek, and the pain kept my mind from dissolving under his words. My own power seemed to buck under his attempts to sway me. I clung to it for all I was worth.

"I don't *have* to do anything!" I yelled.

I flicked the neoprene knife sheath open and grasped the smooth bone handle. Jerking it out, I plunged it into Luke's thigh. He let out a howl and stumbled backward as I turned and sprinted into the surf, slipping my knife back in its sheath as I ran.

"Protect your sister." Grandpa's words rolled through me, a command I was not inclined to ignore.

"Ashling!" I shouted as I ran through the shallow surf, jumping little waves in an attempt to move faster. Fear for my baby sister rolled over me —stronger than the fear I had of the water and what lay beneath it, though just barely. The ocean was not warm, and it stole the heat that Luke's kiss had infused me with. Finally, the water was too deep to run through and I dove in, slicing underneath the surf as a wave rolled over me.

Memories of the last time I'd swum and did my dive, nipped at my heels. I did my very best to ignore them, but they caught me between diving under the waves and surfacing. *The bite of a shark on my leg. The fear I swam to the surface alone in the water, hunted by something that would eat me alive.*

Breaking the surface, I gasped for air and nearly turned back as I imagined all the things that swam below me. Paralyzed by my past, I couldn't move forward. I couldn't go back. Treading water, I trembled, my breath coming in short, sharp gasps. Heart hammering, my vision blurred as I struggled to get enough air, my body shutting down as the panic set in full force.

A wave rolled and in the valley of it was a flash of white. In my mind, all I could see was the white belly of the shark as it rolled with me in its mouth.

Nothing but fear filled me, and I couldn't think straight. I couldn't think, couldn't hardly breathe, as I turned and swam back to shore, sobbing. Waist deep I scrambled for dry land. Running in, limping through the surf, Luke reached out for me as if I hadn't just stabbed him in the leg.

Our fingers brushed.

Something grabbed me around my left ankle.

I let out a cry as I was dragged down and out through the water. Luke didn't follow but stood with his hands in his hair and a look of pure agony on his face. As if it mattered to him that I was about to get killed.

Which made no sense.

The cold water rushed over my head and I closed my eyes. The hold on my ankle was not a bite, but more like a hand, or a tentacle.

Not a shark.

My fear induced stupor broke as suddenly as it had hit, and I fought like a wild banshee, thrashing and twisting, kicking with my free foot at whatever it was that had me in its grip. And then, for no reason I could see, it let go. I swam for the surface.

Breaking the surface, I gasped for air I looked around. I'd been pulled out into the currents. Way out.

Something bumped me in the back, and I spun to try and see it.

A shark. It was testing me out for a meal, like they did. My heart about to burst, I spun again to see Ashling's surfboard. One of her hands gripped the edge of it, white knuckles bobbing in the water, the surfboard actually getting pulled under with her. The sight broke my paralysis. Her head was submerged except for the ends of her hair, which floated on the surface. Something cold and slimy brushed against my legs and I bit down on a scream that made it all the way to my lips before I caught it. Saltwater slipped inside my mouth, gagging me. I spit it out and slid around the side of the board, but not before she lost her grip and disappeared under the water.

"Ashling!" I screamed. My voice echoed out over the water, but the only answer I got was the gulls crying over head, the wash of the waves around us.

Looking down, I couldn't see anything below me. I could barely see my feet. This was no clear Caribbean Sea, but the deep blue ocean. Breathing deep, I prepped myself to dive, but on the second gulp of air the choice was taken from me.

Teeth latched onto my calf yanking me under the water, my hands slipping from the surfboard. The bite was all too familiar. Apparently, I'd been wrong; there *were* sharks in these waters. Serrated teeth sliced through my flesh, biting all the way through the muscle, my foot clamped inside a powerful set of jaws.

My first thought was that Mom couldn't be upset with me now for losing Ashling, not if we were both gone, that was, if she didn't celebrate her liberation from her children. My second thought as I rolled in the water—the pain drawing my eyes to its source—was that I'd lost my mind.

Because it was no shark on my leg.

It was a monster, human in appearance with a single eye set high in the middle of its forehead, and a massive mouth filled with sharp, shark-like teeth. The thing smiled as its hands, hooked like claws, rose up to dig into the waist of my neoprene wetsuit. The jagged tips brushed against my bare skin inside the suit, and I trembled with fear, a new fear. What the hell was it?

"Can you hear me, little Tuatha? I wonder if you know me deep in your soul? We are coming for you. All of you."

I blinked and stared into the huge, soulless eye, felt the keen edge of years behind it, and as much as I wanted to deny what I was hearing, acknowledged that the voice in my head wasn't my own. It was the monsters.

Just like Grandpa had said there would be.

Talking to me inside my own damn head.

What are you? I mouthed into the water, salty brine washing over my taste buds, morbid curiosity overcoming rational sense.

"I am your enemy, the one that will strip your flesh from your bones and bathe in your blood." The voice was masculine, deep and resonant within my head. I wanted to push it out of my mind.

It—he—rumbled and rolled in the water,

taking me with him, end over end like a crocodile rolling its prey until I no longer knew which way was up. Finally, he stopped and began to pull me downward into the depths of the ocean, the water getting colder with each inch we moved deeper. Away from the sun and air.

Air. How could I still be under the water and not need to breathe? As soon as the thought came, it was gone. I didn't have time to think about that, as strange as it seemed.

Movement farther below stole my attention from my own situation. It was Ashling, fighting with a monster very much like the one on my own leg. They were tumbling in the water, her hair floating about like tentacles as she tried to fight the thing off. How could she be in this deep for this long? How could I? Again, that once hollow piece of me responded.

This was why we'd never fit in, these abilities, this magic, these monsters. Though my head said that none of this was real, my heart and soul spoke louder. Grandpa hadn't been crazy.

He'd been right.

This was real, this was happening, and if I was to save Ashling I had to move now. That thought broke through the last of my fear, its hold dissolving within the reality I had accepted.

I grabbed my knife out of the sheath and slashed at the monster that held me in his mouth, slicing through the bulbous eye, in a perfect slash. White fluid reminiscent of smoke poured out of the popped eyeball. He jerked away from me, and released my leg—a spray of my own blood clouding out around me—as he writhed in the water

He screamed, wordlessly, the echo of his pain reverberating in my skull.

Turning my back on him, I swam hard downward, toward Ashling, holding the knife in my mouth. Twenty feet, fifteen, ten. I was nearly to her before she looked up.

She saw me coming and kicked the monster that held her tightly, sending it into a spin away from her. Ashling swam for me, her lips tight, eyes wide and dilated. Five feet. Three. I reached for her, my hand wrapping around her slender wrist. I didn't pause, just turned and started to swim for the surface. Together, we swam hard neither of us looking back.

"She is ours. You will not have her!"

That voice bashed through my skull like a blow to the head.

We were yanked to a stop in mid-stroke, with the surface only a few feet away from us, the sunlight streaming through the waves with tantalizing nearness. I turned in the water and looked down. Ashling had a sea monster on each leg. Her pale green eyes were so wide, they seemed to fill her face as the creatures jerked her from my hands and sped back into the depths faster than a rock sinking. Her hands reached for me, futilely.

Before I could even consider diving down after her, hands grabbed me from the world above and pulled me upward away from Ashling, and out of the water.

"No!" I screamed as I broke the surface, the last of my air erupting in denial. There were people all over the water. Rescuers dove after Ashling. But I knew what they didn't. They would never find her. Somehow, I knew that not only had my sister been stolen by the monsters we'd been warned about, but my world had just shattered beyond repair.

And it was all my fault.

5

"Shark attack? Out here? You've got to be kidding me!"

"Just look at the girl's leg. There is nothing else that bites like that. And the instructor said he saw a fin right before the attack. Not a killer whale either, but a shark."

I turned from the open window outside my private hospital room to see that the source of the whispering was two nurses standing just out in the hall. I'd been rushed to the hospital, my leg bleeding profusely. The paramedics had wrapped my leg and now I was waiting for the doctor to come and stitch me up.

I let out a barking laugh that held an edge of

crazy to it, hell even I could hear the hysteria in the sound.

The nurses spun toward me, their eyebrows raised and their mouths hanging open in unison.

I shook my finger at them as if they were naughty children. "He's lying. There was no shark."

The older brunette pulled it together first, her professionalism coming through loud and clear. "My dear," she said, "what was it that attacked you if it wasn't a shark? Did you see something else?"

I was saved from having to reply by the doctor's arrival.

"Let's get you stitched up," He said as he strode into the room. "Nurse Watkins here is going to help me out. We'll give you some freezing in the leg in a few different places and after that you won't feel a thing."

The nurse hurried to my side and had me roll onto my belly. "You're in good hands, he's got a gentle touch."

I buried my face in the paper pillow, my mind filled with what I'd seen in the water. The weird limbs, the single eyes, the mouth like a shark, but not a shark. I stifled a groan as she lifted the blanket off my leg and started to unwrap the gauze.

"Shh, it is okay," She had barely uncovered the top of the wound when she stopped with a gasp. She regained her composure quickly and pulled the bandage completely off and I twisted around to look. How bad was it?

The bite marks from just an hour before were a mirror image of the scars on my other leg. In fact, they were identical to the scars on my other leg—completely healed.

My mind scuttled back to the dream, of the snake and the pain and the magic that seemed to be hovering around me now. Was this part of what it meant to be quickened? An increase in the speed of how your body healed. I shivered and looked at the doctor.

He stood beside me, his eyes narrowing with suspicion. "Mary, go call Constable Pollett. He'll want to speak with her. You can't lie on record and get away with it."

I didn't understand what was going on. Why would they need the police here? Shouldn't they all be at the beach, looking for some sign of Ashling?

"A shark was it?" he said, a patronizing look on his face. "I see the injuries from a previous attack, but nothing from today."

I had the sudden urge to slap him for his tone and the way he looked down his nose at me. "Look, you're right it wasn't a shark. It was . . ." I paused. I didn't really know what the two monsters were. I had no name for them. And how was I to explain what I saw? They would blame my crazy descriptions on the fear and my past experiences. Or even my family history. Maybe Grandpa wasn't as crazy as we'd thought, he'd warned me about the monsters, and I'd thought he was out of his mind. Or maybe I was about to join him at the pavilion.

In that moment thinking of magic and shark mouthed creatures and being able to hold my breath when I should have drowned, I could feel a sudden urge to offer myself up to just go.

I couldn't though, Ashling . . .she needed me. I didn't for one second believe she was dead.

"It wasn't a shark," I said again, sticking to the one part I knew for sure because I'd seen it with my own eyes. "But it bit me and another one of the same things took my sister. It had arms."

His eyebrows shot up. "Your instructor said he saw the fin of a great white, they do come this far north from time to time, but maybe that wasn't it at all. Perhaps you just got confused when you were tumbled by a wave." His words seemed kind as if they were giving me a way out, but his eyes were dagger-like in their sharpness. What was his problem? "Tell you what, you stay here. We need to give you a full once over before we release you." He flipped the blanket back over my leg, shot me another strange look and walked away. What the hell was that all about?

I sat up and pulled the blanket off my leg. I slid my hands over the identical bite wounds. Healed to the point of looking as if they were months old. "Impossible." I whispered, knowing I'd been bit, knowing I'd seen blood in the water.

"I think maybe you were imagining things," the one nurse said. The other, still in the room nodded.

"It happens when the mind gets overwhelmed by trauma."

They kept talking, slow and quiet as if to a wild animal.

The sound of footsteps in the quiet hallway lifted my head. Luke strolled down the hallway, peered in my door then leaned against the cream-colored wall about ten feet from me. Almost as if he knew I'd take a swing at him if I could. Grandpa had taught me to throw a punch and I was pretty sure I could nail Luke in the chin. He was still in his wetsuit—though it was pulled down to his waist, revealing chiseled abs, golden tanned skin and a chest that any woman would die to have at her beck and call though I was not one of them. He'd held me back, kept me from going to Ashling, even if I had quailed at the last moment. He didn't have the right to try and keep me and my sister apart. His shimmering blond hair seemed duller under the fluorescents and whatever charm he'd used on me seemed dull, or maybe I was just immune to it as my anger surged. The nurses twittered and blushed under his smile. I stared at his leg where I'd stabbed him. There was no wound though the wetsuit clearly showed a slice from my knife. It was as if nothing had happened.

"You son of a bitch!" I said, as I struggled off the bed, scrambling once more for my knife on my waist. The two nurses tried to tackle me, but I pushed them off as I fought my way toward Luke. He didn't seem perturbed at all. In fact, the bastard seemed to be enjoying the show.

The brunette panted as she tried to twist my arm around and under me. The other nurse just grunted as I dragged them both with me like children demanding my attention by hanging off my limbs.

When had I gotten so strong? Again, I thought of Grandpa, and the quickening of me that had happened in my dream. This all tied into the last day's events. My strength, my healing, the ability to breathe underwater. Even fighting off whatever power Luke had tried to use on me. All of it was tied into what Grandpa had done by hurting me. This feeling that I was somehow whole, that all the pieces were fitting inside of me for the first time in my life, even if I didn't understand why.

"Leave her to me," Luke said, his voice soothing and smooth and his hands warm as he gripped my wrists.

"We should leave her to him," the brunette said, and the other nurse nodded as they stood, brushed themselves off and walked down the hallway, their eyes glazed as if they hadn't just been wrestling with me.

I stared after them. "What the hell, Obi-Wan? What did you do to them?" I tried to wave in the direction of the nurses, but my hands were trapped in his steady grip.

His hold eased on me just a little, softening. "You have to trust me on this, Quinn. I will explain this all to you, I promise. But not here, not now." His eyes bored into mine as if the intensity of his gaze could convince me. I glared at him. Hell, I was tempted to spit in his face.

"You stopped me from saving her. And what the hell did you mean by its better this way? Why in the hell would losing my sister ever be better?" I growled the words, my jaw tight and my hands clenched in fists. His thumbs attempted to work their magic on my forearms, but I would have none of it. I jerked my body away from him, stumbled on my bitten leg as a nerve pinched, and fell to the cold hard linoleum. I bit down on a whimper that tried to escape as my leg throbbed in time with my heartbeat.

So maybe I wasn't as fully healed as I looked.

Luke crouched beside me, though he didn't touch me, his hands spread wide as if to show me he meant no harm. Bullshit. "You were lucky they didn't take you too. If they'd known who you were, they would have gone for you first. To be honest, I wasn't sure that they were even there, but now we know that they have indeed resurfaced."

I stared up at him in confusion, seeking his eyes for the truth, not sure if I could trust him. But if he knew that there were monsters in the ocean then he might be my best bet for an answer. Even if he still hadn't answered my questions and had only given me more wrapped up in words I didn't fully understand. He referred to 'they' which had to mean the one-eyed monsters with the shark mouths. He knew them, knew about them. Was it because he was a swim instructor out here on the West Coast? Somehow, I didn't think that was the case.

I didn't know what to think, could barely grasp what was happening. Nothing—from those things I'd seen in the water to how Luke's kiss had affected me, even the way the nurses obeyed him—had gone right since we set foot on that beach, and Luke was a part of it all.

I made a move to stand and he offered me his hand. Ignoring him, I pulled myself to my feet, stepped back a few feet and slid back onto the bed. My leg ached, even though it had healed on the outside.

That was peripheral to my one thought running through my head. I didn't care what anyone else said, I would not believe Ashling was dead till I saw her body with my own eyes. She wasn't dead, couldn't be, even though the facts wanted me to believe otherwise. Even as the monstrosities had dragged her downward, she'd been alive and reaching for me.

Two police officers came in, and Luke stepped back from me, his face going smooth, and a small line of consternation appearing on his forehead. It actually made him look better, more real and not so otherworldly beautiful.

The officers questioned me about the "incident" and finally the tears came. Sobbing, I told them how she'd screamed for me, how Luke had held me back. In shame, I told them how I'd turned back then was grabbed by something and dragged in.

They wrote everything down and the senior officer, Constable Pollett, asked me one last question.

"So, if it wasn't a shark and you don't have any bite wounds, how do you explain her drowning? It says here that she had her dive certificate, same as you. Have you argued with her lately?" He lifted his pen, prepared to write down any information I gave him.

I frowned. "What are you asking me? Are you implying that I would have something to do with her . . ." I couldn't even say it. I didn't believe she was dead. The words wouldn't come out of my mouth.

Luke stepped closer and I felt a wave of pressure as if the air had suddenly thickened and condensed around us. "It was a shark, officer. I saw the fin, there was blood in the water. What else could it be?" Power rippled through his voice, power that I could feel crawling against my skin, seeking a way in to convince me of his words. I fought it, panicked at what he might make me believe.

His eyes locked with Constable Pollett's while his hand played over my fingers like a concerned friend. Constable Pollett's eyes glazed. He nodded and wrote on his pad. The junior officer just stared slack jawed at the wall, a thin line of saliva dripping from his mouth.

Luke continued to speak, and the power swelled around us, nearly choking me.

"She saw a shark, about fourteen feet. A Great White. They've been seen up this way lately as the tuna are migrating farther north. Uncommon, but it happens," he said. The officers nodded. Even I could see their minds buckling under his power.

"I didn't see . . ." I didn't get to finish the sentence as Luke leaned over and planted his lips on mine, sealing them shut against my denial. Again, the warmth spread through me like a sweet hot drink circulating though my blood. I couldn't help myself. I let out a groan and buried my fingers in his hair, pulling him closer. Like a drug I hated wanting, yet found myself seeking out, I couldn't stop tasting him. There was something in his kiss, something that my body demanded, that I was in need of. The power within me, that I'd felt rise on the beach, responded once more. My blood pulsed as the energy swirled around us.

I hated that I liked how his lips felt on mine, hated that I wanted a piece of him for my own bit of sunshine.

The cops stepped away, chuckling as they left. Though that irritated me, I still couldn't seem to fully release my hold on Luke. I managed to pull my head back, a little anyway.

"Love 'n grief, they bind so quickly, do they not . . . Luke?" A deep voice, heavy with an Irish accent, rippled across my senses. Luke pulled away from me. I kept my eyes closed as I struggled to get my rapidly beating heart under control. Slowly I opened my eyes, blinking several times before the humming energy receded back inside of me once more, and I could see my newest visitor.

Where Luke was deeply tanned and fair, the man who stood across from us had hair as black as a moonless night, skin a few shades darker and a body that looked like it was built for brawling. All of that I saw in a single beat, but it was his eyes that snared me. Violet, not blue or gray, but a true violet. A color I'd never seen in anyone else's eyes that were not contacts.

And those violet eyes, they were pissed. Flashing with anger . . . and was that jealousy I saw flicker through them? Impossible, we'd only just met. Unless he was jealous of Luke.

He stared down at me. "If she'd wanted to go with her sister, you should have let her. The stupid ones should be allowed to kill themselves off. It leaves more room in the world for the strong."

I flushed under his judgment knowing I was of course the stupid one he referred to.

Luke shifted his weight and snapped his fingers, his wetsuit shifting and re-arranging itself until it was a T-shirt and shredded jeans.

My mouth dropped open. That had not just happened. Maybe the monsters had been the tip of the iceberg of craziness crashing into my life. No, no I was not crazy, I knew what I'd seen, and I knew exactly what it was no matter how strange.

Magic. Fricking magic.

I shook my head then rubbed my face. This whole day had to be a dream. It couldn't be really happening. In a few minutes, I'd wake up, and Ashling and I would still be in our hotel room, ready to start the day. I shook my head again, and my fingers found the bone handle of my knife.

No, I knew this was happening. I couldn't deny it and pretend that a good sleep would make it all go away. Even if all of it scared the shit out of me. My fingers flexed around the bone handle, there was some comfort in having a weapon, small as it was, with all that was happening.

"What are we going to do with her, Bres?" Luke asked. "We can't take her with us, she'd be in danger. And she isn't ready yet to face the council."

Bres of the violet eyes snorted. "I don't see why we have to be guarding her at all. If the prophecy is true, then she should be able to take care of everything herself. No help needed from us two."

I looked from one unbelievably beautiful man to the other. What the hell were they talking about? "Excuse me, but would you mind not speaking over my head as if I'm a child? What prophecy?"

They continued as if I wasn't there.

Luke pointed at the nurse's desk. "We'll leave her here. She'll be safe with the humans for now. The Fomorii have her younger sister, Ashling. That should appease them, at least for the moment. Agreed?"

Bres scowled and nodded. "Fine but know that I'm only doing this because there be no other way. I don't have to like the job or her." He pointed at me with a thumb.

I'd had enough of this. "Stop ignoring me!" I yelled. They both turned to stare at me. "Tell me what's going on! Who took Ashling? Who are the Fomorii?"

My voice rose with each word, fear, panic and anger vying for my attention, my knife still gripped in my hand and I lifted it, using it to point at the two men. Maybe that would get their attention.

It got attention, just not the kind I wanted.

The noise drew the two nurses back to my room. They saw the knife and the pair of them screamed for the two RCMP constables. This, of course, brought the police down the hall and into the room at a run.

I didn't fight them.

In a few brief moments, they had me pinned to the bed despite my struggles. Luke and Bres were pushed out, though they didn't seem to resist all that much either, as the chubby brunette nurse jabbed me with a needle.

"No, don't sedate me!" I yelled, knowing that I needed to stay awake. I had to get back out to where Ashling had gone under the waves, I had to find her.

The words tumbled out of my mouth, "I have to find her" on repeat as the world went fuzzy around me. My eyes closed as the sedative kicked in and dropped me unceremoniously into unconsciousness.

6

I floated in a world of fog from the sedation the nurses had given me. The smell of the hospital was replaced by the smell of the ocean, the bite of the wind. Dreaming, I was dreaming.

I blinked a few times and brushed my hair out of my face. There were waves and rocks, a stretch of sand out to either side of me and the water in front. I was on the beach again. I took a step forward to get closer to the water.

But this time, I couldn't get to the ocean and it had nothing to do with Luke holding me back. One step and I thumped into something. I lifted a hand and pressed it forward, pushing it against what was an invisible barrier between me and the ocean.

My instincts were telling me that if I could just get to the water, I could find Ashling. A boat, a dive suit and a damn spear gun and I'd be there. I'd get her out.

My hands slid over the slick, transparent surface cutting me off from the water, but no matter how I pounded and screamed, the barrier held firm.

Worse than that a head bobbed out in the surf; blonde hair somehow visible even at that distance.

"No, not again," I whispered as I pressed against the barrier, pounding it with the flats of my hands. Ashling was out in the water, her screams reaching me even though I could not reach her.

"Quinn! Quinn I'm trapped, help me!" Her voice was strained to the breaking, the weight of unshed tears thickening the words.

Panic clawed at me. She needed me, and I couldn't get to her. "Ash, I'm trying! I'm trying!"

Voices whispered across my ears, pulling me out of the fog, but I still couldn't open my eyes. The water and the sand receded, and the hospital smells curled up my nose once more. The nurses were talking.

"We gave her three times the usual dose. She burned it off in a matter of minutes. If we didn't have the steady drip of sedative on her, she'd be awake even now." A shuffle of feet, the blanket pulled tightly around my body as if someone was tucking the corners in.

"What about their parents?" a second voice asked. The doctor I thought maybe.

The first person, it sounded like the brunette nurse, made a hushing sound. "Not so loud. Father isn't around. Their mother . . ." More feet shuffling, and my ears strained to hear what was said.

". . . can't reach her. Went missing today too. So tragic."

My heart picked up speed and the sedative seemed to fade a little more. My mother was missing? She'd only just left for Ireland three days ago, right before Ashling's graduation. I struggled upward through the sedative and opened my eyes to an empty room. The nurses were gone. Like moving through thick mud, I raised my left hand, the IV hanging from it.

I fumbled for it with my other hand and yanked the drip out. A hiss of pain escaped my mouth as the hospital tape pulled on my skin and hair. A trickle of blood dripped down my arm from the injection site but even as I watched, the wound closed.

Right in front of my eyes, the needle wound closed.

Within moments, my mind began to clear. They probably hadn't given me as strong a dose as they thought, then again, I was healing stupidly fast.

Still, I took great care as I sat up and slid from the bed, my legs wobbly underneath me. I had been dreading phoning Mom. How did you tell someone that their daughter was . . . missing? Dead? I didn't even know the answer to that. I think I was most afraid that she'd be happy. I didn't think I could handle that.

The police would say Ashling was dead and that they were trying to recover the body, but I just didn't believe it. I didn't think that Luke and Bres thought she was dead either, and for what it was worth, that brought me some strange comfort. I'd seen what had dragged her down into the depths. It hadn't been a shark or a killer whale. It had been a humanoid creature with a single eye and a mouthful of teeth.

I sat back on the edge of the bed and considered everything that had happened from the moment Grandpa had wrapped his fingers around my neck. The voices in my head, the feeling of finally having all the pieces of who I was fit together, the dream with the snake where if I was honest, I think it had been Luke's voice there too, then the monsters in the water. Luke and the power he displayed, the unreal beauty of both Luke and Bres.

Either I accepted that I'd been inducted into a world I had never known—one with magic and monsters, where even I, the daughter of a woman who didn't want children, had power—or I accepted that I was losing my mind and that all of this was just a psychotic break. There was no middle ground.

Which was it going to be?

Ashling was the tie breaker. If I accepted I was losing my mind, then Ashling was dead.

I would take magic and monsters if it meant Ashling had a chance of being saved.

It seemed that Grandpa's stories and ramblings were true, and maybe they would be helpful. Now that I'd seen a monster for myself, I couldn't doubt they existed. They'd stolen Ashling away like some horribly twisted fairy tale.

Fomorii. The word whispered across my mind

and with it came a shard of anger. That was what had taken Ashling. Luke and Bres had spoken of them as if they would be satisfied now that they had my sister. "We'll see about that," I muttered. "I'm coming for you, Ash."

Across the room, my bag sat on the side table, a rumpled pile of mine and Ashling's clothes within it. The gapped-back hospital gown slithered to the floor, and the air conditioning lifted goose bumps all over my body. Moving fast, I slid into my jean shorts, tank top, and flip flops. My cell phone was there too. I tucked it into my back pocket.

It wasn't much, but it was better than the gown, and far better than being naked as I made my escape from the hospital. My knife was missing, and my heart lurched. It had been my first real and now last gift from Grandpa. For all that he been hard on me growing up, holding me to a higher standard, I cherished that knife.

There was nothing I could do about it now though. No doubt the police took it, maybe as evidence against me?

My mind began to pick up speed as I moved around. I would have to get a boat, maybe hire someone to take me out to where Ashling had disappeared. Scuba gear, I could rent that, though my heart nearly ran away at the thought of diving again. Slipping the bag over my shoulder, I put my hand on the door.

An image of the gaping mouth and bulbous single eye of the Fomorii and his gaping shark tooth filled mouth assaulted me, and a shiver of fear rippled down my spine. A spear gun for sure was going in the gear. That should be on my list too. Maybe I could hire some divers to go with me. That would be best. The water terrified me, but for Ashling, I would do everything I could to save her.

I made my way down the hallway, my leg still aching. At the nurses' desk, I paused to see that they were engrossed in a cribbage game. With their attention on their game, they didn't notice me as I walked right out of the hospital.

The doors slid open with a shush and I stared out into the open parking lot.

The fog from my dream seemed to have followed me into the waking world. A heavy gray mist lay over the world, blocking much of the trees and road from sight. I shivered in the late afternoon air and wrapped my arms around myself. You would have never known it was almost July with the damp air and coolness that it lent to the land. For just a moment it looked and felt like winter was coming on instead of August.

I pulled my phone out and whispered thanks to the heavens that it still had some battery left. I dialed my mother's cell phone in the hopes that what the nurses had said was wrong. It rang four times and then went to her voice mail. I hung up before the message came on. I tried my cousin Sheila which was who my mother had been staying with. No answer there either.

The next number I called was for a cab. The dispatcher, in a completely uninterested tone, finally told me it would be about five minutes. I hung up, and made my way to a cement pillar, leaning against it to ease the weight on my leg. Still sore, even though it was healed.

So much weirdness.

"You shouldn't be out of the hospital yet."

I turned to face Luke, not really surprised to find him there. "I hate hospitals." Not a lie. I didn't like them, but then who did?

He stepped close and I remembered his wetsuit shifting, how he'd made the nurses and cops do what he wanted. He had magic, that much was obvious, and the closer he was to someone the more he seemed to be able to control them. My gut reaction was that he wasn't human, he couldn't be. And if he knew magic, and what I was feeling inside me was somehow answering him, I needed him to help me understand what was going on. At least for now. Time to buckle down and ask the question that had been on the tip of my tongue. "You aren't Fomorii, I can see that much since you don't look like them. So, what are you?"

"I am Tuatha de Daanan, the same as you," Luke said. "Bres, she wants answers."

Bres stepped out from around the cement pillar to my right. "She's going to be a problem for us, isn't she?" he asked.

Luke chuckled. "Are you surprised with her family line?"

Bres shook his head. "Nah, not really."

I hated not knowing what was going on and that they were holding out on me. And what the hell was a Tuatha de whatever anyway?

The word was strange and familiar at the same time, as if I'd heard it before and had forgotten. Like the word Fomorii it stuck in my head.

I was about to ask them what they meant about my family lines causing trouble when the low rumble of a big truck working its way toward us made me look at the road. I frowned as I stared into the fog for the rig as the rumbling grew in intensity and then ground below me bucked. This was no truck; it was an earthquake. The world shivered and swayed, the ground shifting like a tilt-a-whirl making my legs feel as though they were made of jelly.

I jerked my arms out to the side but still fell, my bitten leg not holding up under the rolling movement of the ground below me. My eyes widened at an alarming rate when *both* men leaped toward me, catching me before I could hit the ground. How had they moved so fast?

The quake's rumble and the ensuing heaving of the earth lasted for only a few seconds and then the world was still once more. Though to be fair, it felt longer.

Luke's hands seared my skin on one side of me and Bres's hands cooled the fire on the other—and somewhere in the middle where I stood, I began to melt from the intensity of it all.

"Do you get earthquakes often?" Luke asked me, his face tight with concern. He kept his hands on my waist and Bres stepped away, a glower on his lips.

I shook my head and pulled myself out of

Luke's hands. "Not often until just recently. The island has been hit with them a lot more lately."

I opened my mouth to ask about my family line, but the engine of a car tipped my head around.

The taxi I'd called pulled up and I stepped up to it and slid in quickly. As much as the two men there could answer my questions, I also knew in my gut they would never agree to let me go back out on the water to find Ashling. "Take me to the Wickaninnish Inn," I instructed the driver, locking the door behind me.

"We will be coming with you whether you like it or not, Quinn. You are our charge," Luke said through the open window as he tried the front passenger door. It was locked, and I smiled up at him as he frowned down at me. As if he didn't understand how I could possibly lock him out.

Arrogance, thy name is Luke.

"I need a few minutes to myself. You can meet me at my hotel," I said, my voice hard and clipped though I still smiled. "Maybe that will give you a few minutes to decide it's better to be honest with me instead of playing games."

I gave a nod to the cabbie and he pulled away

from the curb. In the rear-view mirror, I glimpsed Luke with his hands on his hips, and Bres beside him with his mouth in a hard line, his jaw tight with anger.

I spun in my seat to stare as they turned toward one another, and not because they were in a good mood. Luke shook his head and jammed a finger into Bres's chest, and Bres got right up into his face, arms above their heads in obvious irritation.

"Do you want me to go back and get your boyfriend?" the cabbie asked.

"He's not my boyfriend," I said, just as Luke turned to meet my gaze, his baby blues trying once more to snare my gaze. Heat flooded through me as if his lips were caressing mine. My body reacting to the memory as surely as if it were happening right at that moment. I swallowed hard and sat back in my seat. I steeled myself against Luke and the effect his kiss had on me. My focus had to be Ashling.

Besides, it was Luke's fault she had gone down under the water. He'd held me back. I wrapped my arms around myself, shuddering, the image of her reaching for me flooding through my mind.

When the cab stopped in front of the hotel, I tapped the driver on the shoulder. "I have to run up and get some money. I'll be right back." He gave me a smile as I stepped out of the cab.

From where he'd stopped, I could see Chesterman beach and the sound of the waves was a lulling shush against the long sand beach. I gritted my teeth, swallowing the grief that threatened to overwhelm me.

The manager let me into my room since my key card had gone missing somewhere between the beach and hospital. He handed me a new card and put a hand on my shoulder as he opened the door. "I'm so sorry about your sister. She was a beautiful girl. You can have the room here an extra night, and there will be no charge for your stay." His brown eyes were full of sorrow and compassion. They nearly undid my resolve to stay strong.

"Thank you," I managed to choke out. The thing was, no one else was going to save my sister, certainly not the two men who knew what was going on with the Fomorii and the Tuatha. Certainly not my mother. And I doubted the police were equipped to deal with monsters.

"Thank you," I said again as I slipped into the room and closed the door with a soft click.

I gulped down a sob and covered my face with my hands. My phone vibrated in my back pocket and I pulled it out. It was a text message from my cousin in Ireland, Sheila.

Quinn. I don't know if you heard yet, but your mother is missing. Did she contact you? I been out looking all day for her.

I quickly texted back. **No. Ashling is missing too.**

There was no response to that, not right away. Then the phone rang, and I pushed the talk button, the tears spilling out of me before I even properly answered.

Sheila was crying, I was crying, and somewhere in the middle of the tears she gulped out that she was on her way to me, booking a flight as we spoke.

"No," I said, sobering up, wiping away the tears. "Stay there—my mom, someone has to look for her. I'll go after Ashling. I think . . .I think I can find her." Of course, I didn't explain that everyone else thought my baby sister was dead. Nor did I acknowledge the deep fear that was rooted within me: that I was alone, that both my sister and my mom were both gone, beyond my reach. Even though Mom had ignored us, she was still our mother, and I loved her in spite of how we'd been raised. In spite of the fact that I didn't think she loved me.

I said goodbye, as I ran back downstairs with cash clenched in my fist for the cabbie. The manager stopped me at the desk, lifting his hand.

"I paid your fare. It was the least I could do," he said, his kindness surprising me.

I nodded and whispered, "Thank you. I seem to be saying that a lot."

"The world needs more kindness," He said, "Especially when it feels like everything is wrong."

Throat tight I couldn't answer him as I turned and went back up to the room.

I stared out the windows easily finding the very spot where Ashling had disappeared. The world was a darker place without her. I could feel it hanging on me like a shroud of muted colors, sights, and sounds. Ashling was such a huge part of my life, my world, that the thought of her being gone forever . . . it was overwhelming. My body trembled as I stood, staring at the water. No, I couldn't let this be the end. I sucked in a deep breath and cleared my mind.

Trading my shorts for jeans, I slipped on a light long sleeved shirt and headed down the stairs to the paths that would take me through the forest and out to the beach. The pathway was silent, without even a single bird call to help me feel less alone. I didn't know how long I had before Luke and Bres showed up, but there was no doubt in my mind that they would.

They were as tied to Ashling's disappearance as the monsters who'd taken her.

Around me the heavy boughs of cedar and fir, evergreens and maple trees not only lined the wooden path but filled it with the smell of growing things and life. Ferns, moss and flowers I thought were bleeding hearts covered the marshy ground in between the trees. Soon I could hear the surf, the wash of waves on the sand, the hiss of the water pulling back into the ocean with each wave—and for a moment, I hated it all. The world should not be the same as it always was with Ashling gone, with my mom missing.

Except for my life, everything was just going on as normal.

The pathway I was on opened up in a panorama that displayed the shoreline in all its natural glory. The mist had finally burned off with the afternoon sun giving way to the blue sky, blue water and pale sand. I took a step, hit my head on something and bounced backward.

Blinking furiously, I lifted my hand and pressed my palm forward against a barrier that I could not see but was most certainly there.

Just like my dream, I was stopped from getting to the water.

From getting to Ashling.

7

The same barrier that had been in my dreams, keeping me from getting to the water was now *here* in real life keeping me from getting onto the beach.

My hands slid up the slick surface as I searched for an edge, for a way around it. Something.

"No, this can't be happening," I whispered as I stared through the barrier. I could see the sand and water, the brilliant yellow police tape that circled the area where we'd been, pieces of it already down. As if in mere hours the police had given up on Ashling. There wasn't even a police boat out in the water.

There had to be a way around this. I wasn't giving up. I put my hand against the invisible barrier and slowly walked parallel to the beach, my heart rate and breathing skyrocketing the farther I went, the more I realized that it was unreachable. There was no edge.

I picked up speed, running and pushing my way through the bush, the barrier preventing me from even setting one foot on the sand.

This was not happening! Stupid that I could think of no other way to express my frustration, but I was beyond rational thought. I had to get to the water, to find a way to the docks and the boats that could take me, and my dive gear out in the surf.

Maybe I could break it?

I skidded to a stop, searched the ground and found a good-sized rock. With all my weight behind it, I slammed the rock into the barrier, the shock of the impact rippling down my arm, but there was nothing else. Not even a hint of a crack as I slid my fingers over the spot where I'd bashed it.

I was stronger now, stronger and faster and even with that I couldn't break this barrier.

Anger and fear whipped through me and I fell into a frenzy. Over and over, I bashed at the unseen barrier until the rock grew impossibly heavy, my arms exhausted, nails chipped and fingers bleeding. Sliding to the ground, the green moss beneath my knees cushioned me as I choked on the sobs.

I placed both palms on the slick invisible surface, blood from my fingers marring it as I stared at the ocean. A tingle at my back that felt like the warmth of the sun told me I'd been found.

"You won't get her back. You do know that, don't you?" Luke's voice had none of the power in it he'd been flexing before.

I turned my head to look at him. His eyes were sad, even though he'd been the one to hold me back. But I knew that he knew something about where Ashling had been taken. He knew all about the Fomorii. He knew they were monsters.

"Please, she's my little sister. She's alive, isn't she? Tell me that much."

He looked out at the ocean and I thought he wouldn't answer me at first. "She is alive."

A whoosh of air escaped me. Ashling was alive which meant I had a chance to find her, to pull her out of the darkness.

"You know where she is, don't you? You can help me," I said, my voice cracking, tears pooling in my eyes.

His jaw tightened and he didn't look me in the

eye but kept on staring at the water. "I won't help you in this, not to get you through the barrier. Quinn, I'm here to protect you, even if that means from yourself. That is my task, and I cannot veer from it." He stepped forward, crouched next to me and put a hand on the barrier, staring out at the ocean. He was locked out too? "The depths are beyond dangerous. Those that live there will steal your soul if you let them. But the prophecy it. . ."

I stared at him, waiting for him to explain himself further. Waiting to hear the whole story and not just bits and pieces. His eyebrows furrowed down over those blue eyes that had no equal in nature.

"I will guard you tonight. So, there is no fear of anyone coming upon you." His eyes roved up and down my body, a flush of heat following where his gaze touched. "If you have need of me, call out my name and I will come to you." His voice rippled over my skin, promising more than protection. Skin hunger, the desire to be touched and held, lit within me, shocking me with its intensity. No, I would not fall for it. He'd held me back from saving my sister.

He'd told me to let her go.

"Why won't you tell me what is happening,

what is really happening? The police aren't even looking for Ashling, why not?"

He looked away from me. "The human police need to be kept out of this for their own protection."

Human police. My brain was processing his words as he kept on talking.

His eyes swept back to mine. "You need time to embrace this on your own terms, Quinn. No amount of persuasion will make you believe that this is real."

I snorted and smacked my hand against the barrier with a sharp snap to make my point clear. "Believing isn't an issue, Luke. I *believe* this is happening, I just don't understand it. Or why it's happening to me and Ashling."

His hand rested on the barrier and I could almost see him thinking. He tapped the barrier. "This is a barricade put up by the Fomorii. You won't be able to get through, no matter how you try, it keeps all the Tuatha out. The Fomorii are enemies of the Tuatha and you are at the center of a very old prophecy," he said. "More than that your life is in danger. It is why I was sent to watch over you."

He plucked a fern and started to peel it. "I don't

want you to hate me, Quinn, so what I share with you now is something I have not told many people. But I want you to understand why I stopped you from going after your sister."

I frowned and leaned against the invisible barrier, wrapping my arms around myself. "I'm listening." I would give him no more than that.

Luke let out a sigh and scrubbed his hands through his hair, which made the ends spike up in all directions. He looked very young at that moment and a small piece of my anger softened.

"I had a younger brother. He was..." Luke looked up, his eyes going distant, a smile tripping along his lips, "he was my best friend."

A tremble started through me. I suddenly didn't want to hear this story, instinctively knowing how it was going to end. Luke had used "was," past tense in reference to his brother. Which meant his brother was no longer here or was no longer his best friend or both.

I started to stand, and Luke put his hand out. "He fell in love with one of the Fomorii women, they don't all look like monsters, and he sided with them in a battle."

"I don't know if I want to hear this," I said, but he went on.

"He fought me on the field of battle, his woman at his side egging him on to kill me. I didn't want to hurt him, and I did my best not to," he said, his voice thick with sorrow. "In the end, it didn't matter, the hold the Fomorii woman had on him was stronger than his love for me, his brother. I killed him, Quinn. Defending my own life, I killed him."

I sucked in a sharp breath and stared at the man in front of me, who I barely knew, and found myself reaching out to him, to take his hand, his sorrow softening my anger further. "I'm sorry. I can't imagine." I asked.

Luke's hands flexed around mine and I wondered if he thought he held the weapon that killed his brother. "I killed him, and that grief, that all-consuming sorrow . . . I don't want that for you, Quinn. I live everyday knowing *I* ended his life. When I was supposed to protect him."

His words took a minute to settle into my head. I pulled my hands back from him, a cold chill settling over me in the shadows of the forest.

"What do you mean you don't want that for me?" I whispered.

"Part of the prophecy is that you will kill your own sister. That in battle, you will end her life as I ended my own brother's life. I didn't want that for you. I know that pain . . .I thought if she disappeared that maybe you wouldn't have to face it." He kept talking but I didn't hear the words, all I could hear was Grandpa screaming at me.

YOU WILL KILL HER, YOU BITCH.

Nausea rolled and I scrambled away from him as if it were his fault, as if Luke was the problem. But it was me I couldn't get away from. "No, you don't know that!" I threw the words at him. My body shook with fear, anger and grief and utter horror. What he was saying, none of it was true, it just wasn't.

I was up against the barrier as far from Luke as I could get.

He held a hand out to me. "It's better that she's gone now, Quinn. Trust me, you don't want that part of the prophecy to come true. As hard as it is for you now, it is better that her life is ended by the enemy, and not by her sister." He let out a deep sigh while I stared at him, dread filling me. He meant that they would kill Ashling. That if they hadn't already, the Fomorii would kill her.

She might be alive for the moment, but how long did she have?

"We will stay here a few days while I line up

the council. They aren't prepared for you yet. Or me for that matter." His lips tugged up in a rueful sad grin. "The council doesn't know I'm here yet and when they figure it out, I'll be in trouble, but it was worth it, to be here for you."

His smile slipped, and melancholy filled his eyes. "It will also give you some time to grieve her loss, to say your goodbyes. I *am* sorry, Quinn. Please believe me that if there was any way around this, I would offer it to you." He reached for my face and I turned away from him. I didn't want him to touch me right now, could barely think of the words I would hurl at him.

No, it wasn't his fault that this prophecy said I would kill my sister, it wasn't his fault. But he was the messenger and I couldn't help but direct my anger at him.

He let out another sigh. "I will see you later."

Out the corner of my eye, I watched him stand and walk away, toward the path that led up through the forest. In a flash the trees and greenery swallowed him up as if he had never been there with me, as if he weren't real. I turned my head and went back to staring out at the water, hearing it, even tasting the spray as it splashed on the rocks as the wind brought it to me. But I could go no closer than where I sat.

What the hell was I going to do? I couldn't afford to stay at the hotel for more than the free nights they'd given me.

From what Luke was saying Ash was on borrowed time, an unknown amount of time left to her.

I wasn't leaving until I had her back. Decision made, I nodded to myself and stood.

Going slow and I tested the barrier at every step as I made my way back to the Wickaninnish. The manager—John—looked up as I came in.

"The police were here, looking for you, Ms. Lorcan. They asked you to call them when you came back. Something about leaving the hospital without doctor's orders." John lifted an eyebrow as he handed me a business card for the RCMP constables that were looking for me. I took the card and tucked it into my pocket. He gave me a soft smile.

"I'll go call them back in my room," I said.

John nodded. "I'm sure they're just checking up on you, to make sure you're okay."

I flipped the card over in my fingers. "Yeah, that's probably it."

Pulling my phone from my back pocket I checked it as I went back to my room.

There was a text message I'd missed from Sheila.

They found your mother's rental car in a deserted parking lot at the beach with nothing around for miles. The police suspect foul play.

Tremors racked my body, my heart squeezing painfully with each beat. I let myself into my room and walked to the window and looked over the edge at the ocean. I just couldn't look away, I kept hoping I'd see Ash out there.

I called my mother's cell phone again, on the off chance that Sheila was wrong, and my mom had just turned the phone off—that the police were wrong, and she'd just taken a left turn when she should have gone right. She was terrible with directions and a map, so it was possible.

The voice mail picked up. "Hello, you've reached Darcy Lorcan, please leave a message. I'll get back to you as soon as I can. Maybe sooner if I like you lots." Her words trailed off with a laugh and the beep sounded. I hung up and called again, just to hear her voice, just to let her laughter wash over me. Tears streamed down my face as I redialed the number over and over. As much as I wanted to push her situation out of my head, I couldn't. She was my mom and I loved her as much as I loved Ashling. How was I supposed to choose which one of them to go after?

Of course, I knew the answer already. Mom had said goodbye to us a long time ago. Ash and I were on our own, and whatever trouble my mom had found would have to be dealt with after.

I doubted very much my mom was dealing with shark mouthed monsters.

The thought made me grunt in an approximation of a laugh.

After the seventh or eighth time I called her number I finally left a message, halting, stuttering through what I had to say. "Mom, it's me. I . . . please call me as soon as you get this . . .there's something bad I have to tell you." I choked up, caught my breath and went on, my voice barely above a whisper. "Please don't be missing. I love you." I hit the end button and put the phone on the desk.

This far away from where my mother had disappeared there was nothing I could do about her situation; I could only focus on Ashling. I closed my eyes, pinched them shut and held my breath for a count of ten. I couldn't help Ashling if

I was worrying about Mom. I let my breath out slowly, and with it, the thought that I could save them both. I was here. Ashling was closest and I would focus on her. Nothing had changed.

"I'm sorry, Mom," I whispered to the quiet room.

The room's phone rang, startling me. I picked it up. "Hello?"

"Ms. Lorcan, this is Constable Pollett. I came by to speak with you at the hotel today, but you were out."

The conversation didn't last long.

"I want to be clear that you believe it was not a killer whale or a shark that took your sister?" He asked.

"Are you still looking for her?" I asked back, already knowing the answer. "I don't see any boats out there."

He was quiet. "No, my supervisor said it was a drowning accident, and that the body would have been swept out to the open ocean." His words were harsh, and I knew that he was trying to get a rise out of me.

It worked.

"You should be out there looking for her!" I yelled into the receiver. "You should be trying to bring her home, not asking me the same stupid questions over and over! What does it matter what dragged her under the water? She's . . ." I choked up hard. I refused to say gone, or worse dead. She was not dead.

Not yet. And only if I didn't find her first.

"Thank you for your time, Ms. Lorcan. I'm sorry for your loss." Constable Pollett said and hung up before I could respond further.

Shuddering I put the old-fashioned phone back in its cradle.

Darkness bit at the edges of the horizon, taking the sun's rays out in chunks between the few clouds, and with it my hopes of finding Ashling tonight were chewed up.

Part of me wondered if maybe the police were right. Maybe it had been a killer whale and I'd been seeing things because of a panic attack. Only that didn't explain how fast I'd healed, my new wounds, the barrier, or Luke magically making his clothes different.

I stumbled away from the window and toward the bathroom where I splashed some cold water on my face.

"Pull it together," I spoke quietly to myself, "For Ash you have to pull it together. Magic is real.

Monsters are real and you have to save your sister."

I lifted my eyes and stared hard into the mirror. Ashling and I were alike in build and riotous curls, and if I squinted my eyes, fuzzing my vision, I could convince myself that indeed I was looking at my little sister. That she was somehow with me here.

I wanted it so badly that, for a moment, I *believed* I could make it happen. And that's when things got weird.

The power I'd felt inside me that had answered Luke's kiss surged upward through my body once more. I felt it move through me, tightening every muscle as it seemed to seek a way out, my skin feeling as if it was filling, stretching as this magic were flowing along the same paths as my blood.

"Holy shit," I whispered, my entire body tingling. I wiggled the tips of my fingers, coaxing the magic there where it prickled and seemed to dance just at the edges of my body. I let out a slow breath. This was happening, this was real.

The room dimmed, lights flickering as the hotel shook with another small earthquake. I jerked my magic infused hands and slapped them against the mirror to steady myself. It was a nauseating feeling with the ground unsteady below my feet, as if my own legs didn't want to hold me up.

"Ash, I am going to find you," I whispered. "I am, just stay alive."

The lights continued to flicker and the rumble slowly subsided. I finally looked up from staring down at the sink. The glass of the mirror danced with blue lights that appeared to be coming from my fingertips and didn't show my reflection at all. I couldn't stop the gasp that escaped my lips as the gleaming surface cleared. No longer was the image in the mirror showing the shower behind me with beautiful white and gold hand-laid tiles, or even my face smeared with tears and grief.

It showed me a dark cell with stone walls that dripped with water and slime. And huddled in the corner of the cell with her bright red bikini was Ashling.

8

I threw myself at the mirror of the bathroom, shocked that I could see my baby sister through it. Though to be fair it was far from the weirdest thing I'd seen since the weekend had started.

"Ashling!" I tapped the mirror carefully, fearful that I'd somehow inadvertently break this connection.

Her head jerked around and she leapt to her feet, scrambling across the stone floor to reach me. Our hands, though not touching, were pressed against both sides of the mirror. I smiled what I knew had to be a stupid goofy grin even as I was crying. She was still alive! I knew it!

"Quinn! How are we doing this? What's going

on?" she asked, her voice distorted and echoing in the stone chamber. And then the words that cut into my heart like nothing else could. "Please get me out of here."

I nodded furiously. "I'm trying to find a way to you. I can't get to the beach, something, a type of invisible wall is stopping me but I'm not giving up. Did they hurt you?" I asked. She had some bruises I could see on her arms and knees, but no major injuries. That didn't mean they couldn't have done other things to her, things I couldn't see.

She shook her head. "No, they just threw me in this cell and locked the door. I haven't seen any of them since they dragged me down here."

"But you're okay? They didn't try to hurt you?" I didn't say the word rape, but she knew what I meant.

"No. None of them touched me like that, they just left me alone," she said. "How are you going to get here?"

"I'm going to get a boat, and a spear gun and I'm going to find you." I said and the hope in her eyes was enough for me to believe that it would happen. That we'd get her out of that cell and home with me.

I opened my mouth to say that she just needed

to hang on until I got there, to fight with all she had, but she beat me to the speaking part.

"They got Mom too," she whispered. "I saw them drag her through past my cell. I don't think she saw me though. I . . .I didn't even call out to her, Quinn."

A pit opened up in the center of my stomach. It was almost worse than if Mom had been taken by humans which of course was my thought. At least the police would have had a chance in finding her then. As it was, they were both depending on me to save them.

Mother of God help us all that it was on me to save them both.

"I'm so afraid, Quinn. Please, please don't leave me here." Her voice cracked.

I wanted to close my eyes, but didn't dare for fear that if I did, Ashling would disappear. "Never, I will never leave you behind. You have to know I won't. But I can't figure out what's going on."

"It's like so many of Grandpa's stories. The ones about the monsters, the ones he was so afraid of. I thought he was crazy, we all did," she whispered. "I wish I'd believed him." Her green eyes spilled over with tears and her bottom lip trembled hard.

She'd gotten a lot more of his stories than I

had, and I realized this was my chance to figure some of the stuff out.

"I wish I'd believed him too. But he didn't tell me many stories. Do you remember him talking about Fomorii or Tuatha?" I asked.

Her eyes brightened and she dashed the tears away. "Yes! They were the fae that battled over Ireland. The Tuatha were bright and beautiful and kind, sometimes they called them the Shining ones."

"Like Luke," I said, my voice soft. Her mouth dropped open.

"He's one of them?"

I nodded. "Yes, but keep going. I don't remember these stories of Grandpa's. He was always like 'here's how to fight' or 'use your smarts girl'."

"He never told them to you," she said. "Grandpa told me that it would be my job to tell them to you one day when it was time for you to know about them. . ." Her eyes were wide, and I felt my own face mirror her expression.

"Ashling, tell me everything Grandpa said to you that you can remember. I don't know how much time we have, and I need to understand."

She bit her lower lip for a split second and

then launched into a condensed version of the stories, spinning the tale as fast as she could.

The two races, the Fomorii and the Tuatha de Daanan fought over Ireland. The Fomorii were cruel and tyrannical, and they had oppressed the people of Ireland for hundreds of years. When the Tuatha arrived in Ireland, they battled with the Fomorii alongside the humans, and had rescued Ireland from the Fomorii's monstrous clutches and thus restored peace to the land.

"Both races have great strength, speed, healing and powers with illusions. That's all I remember right now, Quinn," she said. Her eyes were their usual pristine emerald tones, but had bags under them, dark circles that attested to the stress she was under. I wanted to wipe them clean, take it all away from her.

"Why are they here though? Why take you away?" I asked.

"I don't know, Quinn." Her eyes sparkled with tears. "I just want to go home."

A wave of exhaustion swept over me. I wavered, my one hand slipping from the mirror. Ashling shimmered and, for a moment, I saw my amber eyes instead of her green ones.

"Quinn. Don't leave me!" she cried out.

“I’m here,” I whispered, fighting the fatigue that was pushing me down. “Wait, there is one more thing. A prophecy. Do you remember Grandpa speaking a prophecy to you? Luke said something about a prophecy being important.”

She closed her eyes, thinking and I thought she’d give me nothing but then she began to speak with her eyes still closed. “Yes, it went like this.” She paused, a frown creasing her brow with concentration, before she began:

“The line of the snake will bring forth a saving light at the darkest hour. Binding all the realms as one—her sword will strike down the evil that haunts the land and she shall lead the fae to victory. Filled with compassion, her heart will remain pure, loving only the Shining One. Through their union, peace shall reign, and the world will know the fae for all that they are, and her sword will forever be at her side.” Ashling let out a small breath. “I think that’s it, pretty close anyway.”

I licked my lips and tried to cement the words in my head. If this prophecy was supposedly for me, for us, then I wanted to know it inside and out.

“Quinn, do you think you can pull me through?” she asked. It had been the question I’d been avoiding because my gut told me I didn’t have the strength—that I didn't have the knowledge—and if it went wrong . . .

"I don't think so. What would happen if you got partway through and got stuck . . ."? I didn't get to finish my sentence.

The door to her cell opened behind her and a three-legged, monstrous beast I remembered from the water crept in. Its mouth of teeth all too familiar, its single eye glaring at me through the mirror.

"Forbidden!" it screamed and launched itself at me. Where Ashling hadn't been able to penetrate the glass, the monster—the Fomorii—did easily. Its arms shot through the mirror, its clawed fingertips wrapped themselves around my throat, squeezing tightly.

Like I hadn't been strangled enough lately.

I let go of the mirror, using both hands to pry at the thing that had me in its vise-like grip. Ashling's screams echoed through the mirror, though I could no longer see her. The monster's arms were dark green, almost black, and slick with some sort of slime that made grasping it nearly impossible. I floundered, my vision slipping in and out as spots appeared in front of me. At the last moment, I wished for my knife. If I had it, I could at least damage the thing that held my life in its hands.

I could fight back.

The cool bone handle was suddenly in my right hand. I didn't think about how it got there, didn't wonder at its appearance. I gripped it hard and used it to slash at the Fomorii beast in the mirror. The blade cut into the Fomorii's right arm, slicing through it as if it were soft, slimy green butter, right through to the bone.

The Fomorii let out a howl and tried to pull away, dragging me closer to the mirror as the last of my own powers burst out of me, uncontrolled, shattering the mirror. The shards of the mirror cut through the Fomorii's arms, amputating them at the elbows. The two limbs fell into the sink with a spurt of blood. I pried the fingers off my throat and drew in a lungful of air. The cool tang of the ocean had never tasted so good on my tongue. I took another breath and my body flooded with oxygen and adrenaline.

I gripped the handle of my knife and leaned on the counter. Where had the blade come from? I shook my head and looked around the bathroom. There were spatters of blood and shards of mirror all over the counter and the floor. There was no way to explain that to housekeeping.

I moved on autopilot, grabbed the Do Not Disturb sign and hung it on the room's door.

The mess was peripheral though. Ashling was alive, and that knowledge fueled me for the next hour while I cleaned the bathroom. The mirror went into the wastebasket. I would have to pay for that no doubt. I held up the dark green, slimy appendages. "What the hell am I supposed to do with these?" I muttered.

I found a black plastic bag under the sink, and I slipped the arms into it, grimacing each time I had to touch them. Disgusting. I stuffed the bag into the back of the closet. I would have to get them out at some point, but all I wanted right then was to shower and go to bed. I was beyond exhausted.

As the water sluiced down me and I scrubbed off the last of the blood and slime, I went over the next few steps ahead of me in my mind. The monster in the water—the Fomorii that had grabbed me—what had it said?

"Can you hear me, little Tuatha? I wonder if you know me deep in your soul? We are coming for you."

Wringing my hair out, I quickly braided it and wrapped myself in one of the fluffy bathrobes. Luke was a Tuatha and he said that I was too, which meant that Ashling was as well. That would explain why Luke was so sure they would kill her. She was their enemy, as was I. Dropping the robe I slipped into an oversized T-shirt and a pair of soft shorts, I curled up in the bed. My eyelids drooped and I struggled to stay awake. Though my heart and spirit were willing, my body was done in by the day's events. I would be no good to Ashling if I was stumbling around sleep deprived.

Tomorrow, I would find a way through the barrier come hell or high water.

9

I woke in the middle of the night, the moon shining on the water and reflecting in through my windows. It took me a moment to remember where I was, and why Ashling wasn't with me. The day before hadn't been a dream, but a damn nightmare.

A tingle of awareness tickled along the edge of my skin, like when I'd known Luke was behind me in the forest.

A soft intake of breath was all I heard before a body glided forward in the moonlit night, my eyes making out the form as it moved from shadow to shadow.

I sat up and scrambled away from the figure, my mind still foggy with sleep.

"Get out of here!" I yelled as I scrambled to flick the light on, tangling up in my sheets, the image of the armless Fomorii coming for his lopped off appendages filled my mind. Damn, where was my knife? It slid into my hand as if beckoned, and I gripped the handle, not even questioning the how of it.

I found the light and flicked it on, though the bulbs were muted as if the power was low giving the room a sense of twilight. A tall figure stood at the foot of my bed, a dark cape shrouding him from head to foot. I caught the flash of his violet tinged eyes as he tipped his head to the side, as if inspecting me.

A breath of relief flowed through me. Not Fomorii, but one of my apparent guardians checking in on me in a most unusual fashion.

"Bres, what the hell are you doing here?" I said, my fear quickly turning to anger as I lowered my knife. How had he gotten in anyway, I hadn't given him or Luke a key card, or even told them what room I was in?

The dim light illuminated his face under the hooded cloak, and I realized my mistake.

It wasn't Bres.

The stranger lifted his hand and pointed a finger at me. I froze, suddenly unable to move. He took two strides, and before I could even attempt to get out of his way, he had picked me up out of the bed and me pinned against the wall. A sharp pinch of my wrist between his fingers and my knife dropped to the floor.

"Ah, Quinn, so like your mother, if one can look past those eyes of yours." He breathed out the words and they caressed my skin, leaving behind a trail of frost on my cheeks that crackled and stung. I stared into his face a whimper slipping past my lips. He had the same violet eyes as Bres, the same dark hair. He looked as if he could be an older version of Bres, which was disturbing. The only true difference was the pointed teeth that glinted out from between his lips as he spoke.

This one . . .he was Fomorii, I could feel it under my skin. Which meant he was with those who'd taken my sister and my mom.

"Don't you hurt them!" I snarled at him, struggling in his grip the pain in my cheek gone in a flash. My instincts screamed at me to do something, but his hold on me was absolute.

He let out a grunt. "I would never hurt your

mother." He tipped his head again like a predatory bird and stared at me, one brow raised. "You have the look of your father too though. The line of your jaw, those eyes. *That* is a pity. I wonder, do you carry other traits of his? Are you a fool like he was?"

I'd never met our father, never knew him at all. Our mother wouldn't even tell us his name. But that didn't mean I would allow some stranger to bad mouth him. "You have no right to speak of him. You don't know him."

He laughed, power rippling around us and my legs went weak. "I know him better than you, his daughter, does." He let out a sigh. "I won't enjoy this. But it's necessary, for Ashling's sake to keep her from harm."

"Please, let them go."

His eyes narrowed and his hold tightened until my wrist bones creaked, "You don't deserve them. They're *mine*. I am keeping them—Ashling especially—where they're safe from you and your Tuatha treachery." He growled.

I tried again to worm free, if just to stand away from this intensity. "No! I would never hurt her! I love Ashling. She's my baby sister."

The stranger snorted. “Do you know the prophecy? All of it?”

I lifted my chin. “Enough, I know enough, not that it matters. I don’t believe in this stupid prophecy, I would never hurt her,” I said.

“Then how do you explain me? Hmm. How do you explain the Fomorii you saw with your own eyes, the barrier that now stands between you and the ocean? How do you explain the power that even now I can sense rippling through your body?”

His questions told me I didn’t know anything much about the prophecy at all. What did the barrier or my power have to do with it? I gave the only answer I could.

“I don’t know,” I whispered.

The stranger loomed over me. “I should kill you now, but I can’t. Even I am not that cold, even I believe that there is power in each of us to change our destiny. Not to mention, a promise, is a promise and I never give my word falsely.” He lifted his hand to my face and caught a tear on the tip of his finger, staring down at it as if it confused him.

I couldn’t move, spellbound with whatever magic he had wrapped around me. His words only added to the paralysis. What promise was he talking about?

I kept trying. “Please give her back. I’d do anything to have her back, to have them both back.”

“No. You will leave her and become a pawn of the council, already that path is being curated for you,” he said, his purple eyes delving into my own. “I will not have that for her. She has too much beauty. She is too much like her mother. I will keep her for my own and safe from you.”

The room darkened and I could feel him—there was no other way to describe it—begin to draw on his power and it was a dark and fearsome thing that blacked out my world. Maybe he didn’t mean to kill me, but that didn’t mean he wouldn’t hurt me beyond measure.

I did the only thing I could think of.

“Help!” I screamed the word, knowing that if either of my protectors were outside my door, they’d hear me.

The stranger’s eyes snapped away from mine as the door was kicked in with a boom.

Bres stood in the doorway with a freaking sword in his hand, the tip pointed at the cloaked man who held me against the wall.

The stranger looked from me to Bres and back again to Bres. A slow smile spread across his face showing off his sharp teeth. He locked eyes with me once again, ignoring Bres as if he weren't even there.

"You, Quinn, are trespassing on my lands. I will give you until midnight tomorrow to leave. If you are still here, I will consider it an attack on me, and your life will be forfeit regardless of any former promise I have made." A crack like the sound of thunder filled the room and in a swirl of darkness, he was gone. The lights dimmed and went out and I slid to the floor all the wind taken out of me.

I blinked and Bres was crouched in front of me, his eyes hard and his jaw twitching. "Did he hurt you badly?"

I shook my head and rubbed at my wrists, then lifted a hand and touched my still cold cheek. "No, he didn't hurt me, not really. He was starting to draw on his power—what was he going to do?"

Bres gave me a sharp nod. "You did the right thing, Quinn. He was preparing to wipe your memory and steal your power. It would be a sure way to end any role you would play in the prophecy without killing you."

A lump formed in my throat. I didn't doubt

him, not for an instant. If Bres had been a second later or if I'd hesitated in yelling for help . . . I shivered at the thought of all my memories being wiped like a dry erase board.

Of forgetting those I loved the best.

Luke appeared in the doorway, a sword in his hand. Crap, what was it with the weapons?

He did a quick sweep of the room then came to stand next to us. "You can leave now, Bres. I will take it from here."

Bres frowned. "I'm to be protecting her as much as you are, Luke." The two men stared at each other, neither backing down.

I waved my hand between them, catching both of their attentions. "Hello. Listen to me. The guy, whoever he is, has my sister and my mom. We have to find out who he is, where he's got them! Then I can get them out of the cells."

They stared at me as if I was speaking Chinese. Did they not understand how important this was?

"We know who he is, Quinn, and we know where your sister and mother were taken," Bres said. His accent seemed stronger than it had been before.

It was my turn to stare. "You mean you know

exactly where they are? I mean, I know you said the Fomorii had them but—"

Luke held up a hand, stopping my ramble. "That was Balor. He is the ruler of the Fomorii," he lowered himself to sit on the edge of the bed.

"He doesn't look like the others," I said, thinking of the bulbous eyes and slimy black skin the Fomorii I'd already met. Then again Luke had said his brother had fallen in love with a Fomorii who'd been beautiful.

Bres gave me a wry smile and a wink I didn't understand. "The more powerful the Fomorii, the more human they look. Balor looks very human."

"Except for the teeth." I pointed out.

Bres sighed. "Yeah, there be that."

"We can't go after them, Quinn," Luke said, his hands clasped loosely in his lap. "I'm sorry, but the likelihood is they've both been killed already."

I was shaking my head even before he finished speaking. "No, I saw Ashling. She's still alive. And Balor, he said she was beautiful, that he was going to keep her for his own. Does that mean what I think it does?"

Luke and Bres exchanged a look, one that tightened my heart with fear for my sister. "Tell me," I said. She hadn't been harmed, hadn't been touched. But that didn't mean something bad wasn't coming for her.

"She'll become his mistress, if all goes well." Bres lifted a hand to stall me but I barrelled over him, my voice hitting octaves and decibels I hadn't known I could reach.

"If all goes well? Are you out of your mind? That's rape!" Adrenaline and anxiety battled for dominance inside of me, making me vibrate with the need to move. "We have to get her out of there!"

Luke stood; his face drawn with anger. "We can't!" he shouted, his power filling the room, the air thickening until I was pushed to my knees. "It is done and there is no undoing it, Quinn. There will be no more talk of rescue. You cannot go to your sister or your mother."

I glared at him and he glared right back. Bres broke the silence.

"Not to mention the bounty on your head. If you were to step into the Fomorii kingdom you'd be mobbed and killed, eh, Luke?" Bres said, drawing out each syllable.

Luke turned his glare on Bres. "Yes—that would be a problem *if* we were going after them. But we aren't." He paused and lifted an eyebrow at

Bres. “You don’t have a bounty on your head. Would you like to tell Quinn why?”

Bres shrugged, his lips quirking over some joke I didn’t get. “It don’t be bothering me none. You see, Quinn, I don’t have a bounty ‘cause while my ma is Tuatha, my father is Fomorii.”

10

Bres announced he was half-Fomorii and that was it for me. I was done.

"Get out, both of you." I pointed at the door and they surprisingly left without a fuss. Luke even fixed the door, the hinges flowing back into place and then the door shut nicely with a click.

Sleep was out of the question after my rude awakening by Balor.

So, I paced the room in the semi-darkness my brain on overload.

Balor had Ashling. Bres was half Fomorii which made me wonder how I the hell could I trust him? What if he was a double agent? Would he try to kill me for Balor? I crossed and uncrossed my arms several times, agitated and scared. Luke wouldn't help me rescue Ashling, of that I had no doubt. The minutes and my chance to find her were ticking by, the seconds rushing past me.

Maybe she wouldn't be killed but being raped . . .I didn't think that was a whole hell of a lot better.

How long would Ashling have before Balor took her to his bed? What if her temper flared and he decided that her beauty was not worth the trouble? That could get her killed as easily as anything.

"Ashling, just play along a little while," I whispered into the night air. "Fool him and buy some time."

Midnight tomorrow was the deadline and I knew it wasn't enough time. For some reason, I did not doubt Balor's words that he would come back for me. As crazy as the events were, I knew they were truly happening, and they felt like a chess game. But I didn't know all the players or what they were capable of, and I was a single pawn left facing the entire board on my own.

I shook my head. "You will not give up, Quinn," I said. "Ashling and Mom are depending on you."

Protect your sister. Grandpa's words were as poignant now as when he'd first said them so many years ago. "I'm trying." I whispered to the empty room.

An overwhelming desire to leave the room and get some fresh air washed through me, the need to move and do something, anything but just sit there and wait for the time to pass.

A breeze rolled through the room smelling of the forest and I turned toward the door, the sensation that something was calling to me strong enough to draw me out of the room.

Magic was in the air, and I could feel it against my skin.

I scooped my knife up off the bedside table, and the bone handle warmed in my hand. I tucked it into the neoprene sheath and put it over the waistband of my shorts, flipping my shirt over it to hide the get up.

At the door I peeked out but neither Bres nor Luke stood guard, though I had no doubt they'd be close by. Of course, they probably thought I'd be curled up in my bed, sleeping, maybe crying.

Moving at a quick jog, I ran out of the room and down the stairs in bare feet. There was something—or someone—calling me, enticing me to come outside. I didn't feel coerced, only curious and somewhat excited as if I were about to discover a mystery.

Maybe whoever was calling me would be able to fill me in.

Halfway down the stairs, the ground swayed and shook. The chandeliers clanged above my head. I cried out as I was flung against the stairway's guardrails. The quake lasted longer this time, nearly a full minute. And when it left, so did the power. Feeling my way down I made it to the main floor.

The words of the hotel staff and patrons buzzed up around me, so many people woken rudely in the middle of the night. The generator kicked in and the back-up lights came on.

I looked over my shoulder, sure that for a moment I saw the dark head of Bres.

Quicker, I had to move quicker. Through the semi-darkness, I dodged people as if they were standing still, my newfound speed working in my favor. I ran out through the front doors and onto one of the wooden pathways, one that took me deeper into the coastal rainforest. The farther away I got from the hotel and all those people, the more my feet slowed, my mind doing all the racing I needed. Still, the pull of something calling me was there, attached somewhere around my belly button, gently guiding me forward. I wasn't afraid. I didn't think the Fomorii had it in them to be that gentle or careful. They'd made their threat, and I suspected that Balor really was a man, or Fomorii, of his word.

I was deep into the forest when the pulling on me suddenly stopped, but I kept walking, the night air soothing me, cooling the adrenaline and fear a little.

I pulled the blade out of its sheath and rolled it in my fingers. "And what is it about you? Jumping into my hands when I need you? Are you magic too?" I placed it on the ground and walked a few feet away, keeping my back to it. I looked over my shoulder and held my hand out as I put all my will into wanting the blade in my hands, but nothing happened. It lay in the moonlight, the gleam of ivory bone easily visible against the wooden path.

"Trying to get a blade to jump is hard."

I spun, my fingers reaching for my knife, circling around the handle as it appeared in my hand.

"Ha. Impressive. I shouldn't be surprised, not with your bloodlines." The voice was coming from my left and I turned to face it. The voice was familiar, but not one I could easily place.

"What do you mean?" I asked, my eyes searching out the speaker.

"Blade jumping is an old trick. Not one that many use because it takes years of practice. But that's a family weapon, isn't it?" the voice asked. There was a slight tremor to the voice, a faint accent if I listened hard. But it wasn't Irish like Bres's—it was something else, something older.

"Yes, my grandpa gave it to me. It was his and he said I should have it," I said, shifting my feet and trying to determine if this person was going to be a threat or not.

"The knife knows it belongs to you. It is, in a sense, bound to you. When you have need of it, and call for it, the knife will jump to your hand, no matter the distance between you and it. Very important when you face your enemies to have at least one weapon that is bound to you in this way. That weapon will never be turned on you."

A couple strolled toward me, giggling and laughing, their arms woven around each other. Was one of them the speaker? They nodded at me, and I tucked the knife behind my back so they kept on walking, oblivious to the weirdness that was my life.

"Ah, young love. I miss it so," the voice said, letting out a long sigh.

I stared at the couple, but they hadn't reacted to the voice, not even a giggle. They sashayed down the boardwalk.

"Oh, they can't hear me, pet. Only you can hear me. Only those whose fae blood runs strong through them can hear the voice of an old goddess like me." She gave a low laugh that turned into an odd giggle.

I brought the knife back out in front of me. "Are you with Balor?" I asked.

The voice let out a violent hiss and the bushes to my left rustled. "That old bastard. Never! I'm here to help you. Luke and Bres, they make good guards with all their muscle and belief that they can protect you. But they won't guide you. You need a mentor for that." The bushes rustled again, and I took a step back. Then I screeched as a five-foot-long, brilliantly blue snake slithered out of the ferns. Now I knew why the voice sounded so familiar. It was the snake from my dream. The same damn snake from Cathedral grove.

"Oh, hush, yourself. It's a body that is easy for

me to take. My old bones don't pain me when I'm in my snake form," she worked her way over a few rocks to get closer to me. I stared down at her, not sure what to do. The blue of her scales was nearly neon it was so bright with the tip of her tail, and head, a vibrant red to offset it. Not exactly subtle, but identical to what I remembered from my dream. Identical to the snake that I'd seen in the grove and called in to the conservation officers.

Did that mean that Luke had been in my dream as well? I recalled the hands stroking my forehead, holding me, and a delicious shiver ran through me.

"Come on now, pick me up. I'm not slithering after you all night. And if I'm right, you've got a deadline to meet, don't you?" she said. "No doubt you have a very short time to rescue your family."

I swallowed hard. Snakes were not on my list of favorite pets, and I wasn't interested in getting bit by one. But what choice did I have? I needed help, and the two men assigned to me were far from forthcoming in that department. And while she was a snake, she was giving me far more hope than anyone else.

Bending slowly, I put out my hand, holding my breath and biting my tongue. She slithered up to me and made her way up my arm, draping herself over my shoulders as if she'd done it a thousand times. If she was such an old goddess, perhaps she had. I held very still, the cool, dry feel of her belly not unpleasant, but still somewhat unnerving.

"You can call me Cora," she said, her tongue slipping out to taste the air. "It's one of many names that I go by."

I stared at her mouth. "I can't see your mouth move when you talk," I said.

Cora's tongue slipped out again. "It's a projection of my thoughts into auditory tones. I don't need vocal cords to speak. Goddess, remember?"

I nodded as if that made all the sense in the world. "How are you going to help me?"

"Tell me of the deadline. What has happened to bring you here?" she asked.

I started down the path. "I have until midnight tomorrow—today, I guess—to leave these lands or Balor is going to kill me. He said he would consider it an attack on him if I stayed."

Cora's body tightened around my neck and I took a shallow breath. Had I upset her? Was she going to strangle me now?

"Balor was always one for theatrics. If he tried to kill you, his own son would stand in his way before letting that happen. Balor, for all his tyranny, loves his children and those he's lost along the way haunt him." She let out a long sigh and I stepped off the path, my bare feet sinking in the thick moss that covered the forest floor. A sense of the surreal filled my brain and my body as fear rose within me. Ashling and Mom were depending on me and how I played this chess game.

"Wait. You said Balor's son would stand in his way." I thought of the violet eyes on both men, Bres's confession of his Fomorii blood and the twinkle in his eye when he told me about it.

"Bres is Balor's son?"

Cora let out a long sigh. "Yes, though you must not hold it against him. Bres renounced his father and how he treats the fae. It's why he's here helping Luke, though they don't like one another. They have fought one another off and on for a long time." Her tongue flicked out tasting the air. "Bres is a man of his word though, and you can trust him. He will protect you at all costs, even unto his own death."

I mulled over this new piece of information. Bres, though he'd been gruff with me at first, hadn't hurt me. I couldn't put the father and son into the same category.

"Now, sit yourself down. We will discuss what needs to be done and what needs to be known." Cora wrapped herself around me, her tail tucking underneath her coils, making me a perfect serpent necklace.

With great care, I slid my back down the trunk of a tree, planting my butt in the soft ground.

Cora sighed and settled into teach me a few things. "Bres is both Tuatha and Fomorii, as many fae are. It is what you choose for your path that defines which race you will take after. Bres, like others, has renounced the darkness within himself and pledged to help defeat Balor and the Fomorii. That is enough. But remember, the darkness will always call to him. It is seductive in its own way." I thought about what Balor had said, how we made our own choices, to change our own destiny.

Her coils tightened and then relaxed, her red head lifting out in front of me so she could turn and look me in the eye. "Now, on to what you must know, what needs to be spoken to you that the others will not. The barrier will only be the first of the challenges you face. I will help you pass it. You need to rescue your sister. Your grandfather was right, it is for you to protect her."

I didn't know how she knew my grandfather's

words, but I didn't disagree. Even though it brought a spurt of fear through my body.

A chill swept down my spine, shivers of a past that resonated in my soul. Her perfect diamond-shaped head bobbed. "Yes, you should be afraid. Once you are within the Otherworld, you will be forced to fight your way to your mother and sister. And that is only the beginning. The Fomorii hate the Tuatha with a rage that is not equaled anywhere in the history of this planet. They were ousted from the Emerald Isle and believe it was wrongly taken from them. Many Fomorii were killed in the battle and they have a long memory. They will see you as an enemy without any other reason than you are from the Tuatha."

"You're going to help me rescue them? Seriously?" I asked, hope stirring. I ignored the rest of what Cora was saying. I didn't want nor need a history lesson right now.

She gave a flick of her tongue. "Both of you girls play important roles to bringing peace to this land—we need you both alive. Stupid council and their belief that they know the prophecy better than I do. Please, that's the most ridiculous thing in the world."

The wind blew, rustling the bushes around us,

stray strands of my hair catching the breeze. I stared out into the forest. "Why are the Fomorii here, if it was Ireland they were ousted from? Why did they take Ashling and my mom?"

Cora let out a hiss and curled herself back around my neck, her head now underneath my braid. "I don't know the answer to the first question. I could guess but I would not put those thoughts into words, for fear they would come true. As to why they stole the ones you love... that you must find out on your own. I'm here only to help you find the path you must walk and give you the tools you will need to fight your battles."

I sat there, thinking.

"If I am a Tuatha, then so is my mother," I said, trying to wrap my head around all the information I was being asked to not only take in, but believe completely. Weirdly enough, I did believe it. For better or worse I as all in.

"She is only a quarter Tuatha." Cora said. "Your father is full-blooded fae."

I startled. "You knew my father?"

Her coils tightened a moment then released me. "He was a good man."

I pinched the bridge of my nose because as much as I wanted to know more about my father, a man that my mother had never spoken of, it wasn't pertinent to saving Ashling.

These were just details right now—they didn't matter in this moment, not really. It didn't change the fact that I was going after my family. Maybe when this was all over, I could talk to Cora about my father.

Assuming I was still alive.

"I have until midnight tomorrow to get to Ashling and get her out of the ocean, or wherever it is the Fomorii took her," I said. "She's alive now, but I don't know if they won't change their minds."

"Quinn, who are you talking too?" I spun on my knees to face Luke; his brows drawn over his eyes. He stepped into a patch of moonlight which only strengthened the beauty of his face.

"Um. I was just . . ." I waved my hands in the air, then finally pointed at Cora who was wrapped around my neck. She let out a long hiss and flicked her tongue at him.

"Good gods, Corchen. Really? You weren't to come here." Luke's voice and eyes softened with something akin to pity. He shook his head and again I was struck by the sadness that filled his features when he let his guard down.

Corchen? That name rang a bell.

"I don't go by Corchen right now. Last I checked you weren't in charge of me. If I recall correctly, boy. Besides, it was you that wasn't to come here to, Quinn, if I recall correctly. There were no restrictions put on me." Her coils tightened and I tensed until she relaxed. She lifted her head. "No, I think you're just jealous. I'm going to usher her in for the last of her quickening. Not you."

Now that was interesting. Luke wasn't supposed to come to me?

And then her words hit me. I did not want more of that quickening business.

Luke stepped forward and very gently pulled Cora off me though she tried to bite him twice, her strike fast, but Luke faster. "Old lady, you are not fit for these battles anymore."

She coiled around his wrist with the length of her body while he held her just behind her head. "I want to help. I still have some years left, Luke. Don't turn me away from the last of my line. This will be the last fight I see."

I blinked several times as her words sank in. "We're related?" I did not fancy ending up in a snake form.

Luke took a deep breath. "Yes, she is the

founder of your lineage. And you are the last of hers."

"Why did you call her Corchen?" I asked.

He sighed. "Many of the older fae have multiple names. When I first met her, she was Corchen."

The line of the snake. That was straight out of the prophecy.

Cora twisted and writhed around his forearm. "I will protect her with my life, you know that, Luke. Then you will be able to free Bres from his bond so he will not be bound to stay here and protect her, and you will be able to do as you please with whoever you please," she said.

I put my hand out and peeled her away from him, "She can stay with me. I don't mind."

His eyes widened and he lifted an eyebrow. "Fine. But it does not relieve anyone of their obligations. Bres made a promise, he will damn well hold to it."

Cora tightened over my arms, locking them within her coils. A pair of handcuffs made from a serpent. Awesome.

"Hey, what are you doing?" I asked, trying not to get panicky as her muscles tightened around my hands further.

Luke grabbed the end of Cora's tail and began to unwind her. "Corchen, let her go, let her gather her strength before you do this. It's been a rough twenty-four hours."

Cora only squeezed me tighter. "It is her time. I must quicken her blood now. The prophecy calls for it. It is my task as she is one of my own and if I do not do it now, I do not know when we will have another moment of quiet."

I did not like the way this was going, and I wriggled my hands, trying to get them out without hurting her.

Luke continued to unwind her body, searching for her head which she'd stuffed underneath her own coils.

"Don't do it, Corchen. It will only heighten Balor's resolve to kill her. Let her at least speak to the council first. I think that would be better," he said as his hands worked at untangling her body from my arms.

"Quinn will not have a chance if her blood is not quickened. And we both know that Balor will try to find a way to kill her no matter what. This will give her the chance she needs."

"Wait, what are you talking about? And, I think I've already had that whole quickened thing, my grandpa and then the forest dream. . ." I started to explain that I'd already been quickened, by my Grandpa.

Cora didn't answer me, at least not with words. Her bright red head appeared, and before Luke could grab her, she reared back, let out a hiss and struck, her fangs sinking deeply into my neck. I let out a strangled cry and sank to the ground, moss cushioning my fall. Luke's hands caught me before I hit the forest floor and lowered me into the soft moss as my world dissolved in a blaze of fire and pain.

Again.

11

I writhed on the ground, every inch of my skin lit from within, nerve endings firing spasmodically throughout my whole body. Cora had bit me and whatever was in her venom was doing a serious number on my body.

There was no doubt in my mind this was more than just some simple snake poison. Quickening my blood did not sound like a good deal to me, but that's what she'd said and here we were. Me in pain once more.

"Damn it, Corchen, you know what will happen to her!" Luke said, somewhere close by my head.

With every beat of my heart the pain intensified, as if it originated within me and not from the venom in Cora's fangs.

"Then you must protect her. It is what you were born for Luke. That's why I didn't tattle on you to the council even though I could have." Her voice was right in my ear and I had an urge to grab her and break her snaky little neck, relative or not. But my nerve endings were white hot, screaming at me to put the fire out, and that left little room for anything but trying to hang on to consciousness and pray I didn't die on the spot.

As quickly as the pain had hit me, it began to fade, and that strange power that I'd felt well within my body once more rose to the surface, bringing with it the strength to flush away whatever she'd done to me.

"It is as I thought," Cora said. "I dreamed your blood had been quickened by another, that you rode the pain, another in my guise. That is not well done. Well done by you, but not that you faced it alone."

Luke dropped down beside me, his body cradling mine. "Who quickened you, do you know?" he asked softly, his voice right in my ear.

I put a hand to my face, then my throat, no evidence of my grandfather's bruising there.

"Blake, my grandfather," I said. "But in my dream, you were both there."

They exchanged a look I couldn't decipher. "Maybe to make you hate us?" Luke offered to the snake.

Cora bobbed her head. "Luke and I were not truly there, though I dreamed it, as no doubt Luke did too. I just did not realize that it was a dream of truth. I thought what I saw was a foreshadowing of what was to come. You did well, Quinn. You did not try to flee the pain but embraced it. By riding out that fire you will be stronger for it." Cora's voice whispered into my ear as she slid to her spot around my neck. "I am sorry for biting you. My venom is uncomfortable even for those of the long-lived bloodlines. Your grandfather must have wanted for you to have his memories very badly."

"Huh?" I mumbled, Luke's hands drew patterns over my upper arms and his touch was quite literally putting me to sleep.

"When your blood is quickened, you gain the ability to draw on your powers. It's why you were able to stay so long under the water," Luke said. "I should have known then, but I just assumed it was a matter of need, your abilities showing up. That can happen too."

"That's why Ashling could stay under so long too?" I asked.

Luke nodded. "Most likely."

"Along with that," Cora added, interrupting us, "whoever escorts you over gives up their most important memories, the ones they feel the initiate will need in order to thrive. I daresay, he must have thought you needed his memories more than you needed to pass through the pain with any sort of comfort."

"I don't see any of his memories." I said with a frown, closing my eyes as if that would help me see something of Grandpa's past.

"They come when they are needed, and not a moment before." Cora said. "But his memories . . ." Very suddenly she changed subjects. "I am tired, and you need to rest while your blood burns the venom burns. Luke do not misbehave," she said as she tucked her head under her own coils and went to sleep.

I lay on the mossy ground, my head in Luke's lap as the world lightened around us, the sun rising slowly. His warmth feeling not unlike the rays of the sun spread through me and I let out a small sigh. I could lie here forever, his hand stroking my brow, his presence giving me a sense of security that surprised me. I found my hand creeping into his, stroking the soft spot between his thumb and first finger. Why was he really protecting me? Perhaps my lips even formed the words.

"We protect you because you are a light in these dark times, a chance for renewal," he said, answering my thoughts as if they were his own. "You are everything the Fomorii want and cannot have. There is a reason so many of them stole Tuatha women away to be wives and mistresses. In the world of the fae, sex and love are as much their own power as the magic we carry."

Heat flared deep within my belly at the thought of Luke stealing me away, of making me his in truth and images came unbidden to my mind, catching me off guard.

The pressure of skin on skin, of naked bodies that writhed against one another, a glimpse of desire flaring in his blue eyes as I nipped and tasted my way down his bare chest. He pulled my chin up and pressed his body against mine, breath hot against my mouth.

Luke lurched away from me and I rolled to the side, pushing myself up to my feet. If a bit unsteady, I was at least standing. I had to put a stop to that line of thinking.

I glanced up to see him crouched in front of me. Electricity—and I mean true electricity—flared between us, crackling through the air as my power rose inside me answering the call of all this desire. Blue lightning danced across my fingertips as I lifted my hand to touch his. He sucked in a sharp breath of air but didn't pull back, instead weaving his fingers with my own.

I stared into his eyes and the images flowing between us started once more, thick with all the things that shouldn't be, not when we'd only just met.

Hands traced along the curve of my spine, and his fingers rested in the hollow of my back holding me tight to him. My breasts pressed against his smooth chest, so that I could feel each beat of his heart matching my own. I leaned forward and put my mouth to that hollow of his throat his skin fever hot. I pressed my lips and flicked my tongue against that sensitive skin, tasting him as his hands roved over my body, past the curve of my waist, over my hips to hold me tight against every inch of him.

I let out a gasp, my body tight with desire, the intensity between us growing with each passing second. His eyes were locked on mine and even if

I'd wanted to, I wouldn't have been able to look away.

The rational part of me tried to explain that this was not smart, that I didn't really know Luke, nor did I know what games he might be playing. The less than rational side of me told that rational side to shut up and enjoy whatever game this might be because it was about to rock my world.

With great care, Luke unwound Cora from my neck and settled her into a bed of moss behind a log. Placing his finger to his lips and giving me a damn sexy wink, he came back to where I'd sat back down.

Rational Quinn said go back to the room idiot.

Non-rational Quinn stayed right where she was.

Luke curled one arm around my waist and leaned forward so he could nuzzle my neck, nipping his way along my collarbone. "Ah, Quinn, I want you so badly, but the council will want to be sure you are the one the prophecy speaks of. It won't matter to them that I know it in my soul. You belong to me, but we must wait if the prophecy is to be fulfilled properly, or there will be no peace between the Fomorii and Tuatha." His lips made their way up my neck and to my trembling mouth.

I closed my eyes, trying to think past the desire his touch sent raging through me. "You mean, we're supposed to be together, that's part of the prophecy?"

"Yes," he murmured against my skin. "You are the one I've waited for all these years. This is meant to be. You and I."

His lips hovered over mine and I waited for the moment, my body shaking with need, the pulse of his power wrapped around us as tightly as his arms circled me.

A breath was all that was left between us, and my rational brain was still holding me there keeping me from taking that last move, when something razor sharp stung my hand. I yelped and fell backward as Luke did the same, both of us rubbing our hands. Cora coiled up between us, jet black eyes narrowed as she gave Luke what I would guess was the epitome of a snake's glare.

"You'd best let her go, boy, or you will taste my venom a second time," Cora snapped. Pain flickered in my hand, up my arm and then slid away from me. Cora glanced at me. "You will build an immunity to my venom. It will never hurt like the first time, but it will always sting."

Luke's face tightened and he cursed under his

breath. Shifting his weight, he stood, and I scrambled to stand with him, not sure if I was embarrassed or grateful to Cora for cutting the make out session short.

At least that's what I was trying to do. It was as if only the mere thought of standing caused my body to respond in a lightning-fast manner. There was what felt like no time lapse between my thoughts and my actions.

I let out a gasp and Luke nodded. "You will begin to see, Quinn. Like in the hospital, with the rapid healing of your leg, or how strong you were, or how long you could hold your breath under water. This is a gift and a curse to have your blood quickened, and each day you will find more of what that truly means. The moments will come most when your adrenaline is highest." He let out a small sigh and gave me a short, stiff bow. "I will protect you, but I must keep my distance. Otherwise, I cannot be certain I can control myself, about that much Cora is right. I will not dishonor you."

He turned and walked up the path away from me and a pang twisted around my heart. The passion he'd ignited burned hot in my blood and it was far from unpleasant. The safety I'd felt within his arms was something I'd been searching for my whole life. A person who loved me, just for me and who would stand with me.

But did he? That question smacked me up the back side of my head. He'd said that I was meant to be with him, not that he loved me, but that the prophecy said we were to be together.

A lump rose in my throat, emotions I didn't want right now filling me and threatening to spill over.

You helped someone you loved, you did things for them that you wouldn't otherwise do for right or for wrong. I steeled myself to ask that one question.

"Luke, will you help me find my way into the barrier now?"

He paused and looked over his shoulder, then slowly shook his head. "More than ever, no. I cannot protect you if you cross to the Fomorii. And I will not be the one responsible for your death. I have waited too long for you."

His words sent chills through me, and I wrapped my arms around my body, shivering in the weak light that burned through the mist. In a swirl of air and fog, Luke was gone, and I was alone with Cora.

Not love then, but fate. I wasn't sure that was the kind of connection I wanted at all.

I turned back toward the hotel, my body aching from the night's activities. I was suddenly desperate for warmth, food and comfort. A warm blanket, a bar of chocolate and that would take care of all three things.

My feet moved on autopilot, but it wasn't until I was back on the wooden boardwalk that curled through the forest that a thought stopped me. I stood looking at the Wickaninnish and considered how it would look to see a five-foot-long neon blue snake wrapped around my neck and me still in my pajamas as I walked in through the doors.

"That won't work," I said.

"What was that?" Cora mumbled, lifting her head.

"I can't just walk in with you wrapped around my neck. I can hide the knife, its small enough. But you're too big."

She shifted her coils. "I told you, the humans can't see me. You've no fear from anyone on my behalf." Her tongue forked out to taste the air. I doubted that, but then the couple certainly hadn't heard her talking earlier.

Steeling myself for a fight with the manager on

why I was bringing a great big exotic snake with me, I stepped into the front door of the hotel. A quick glance at the counter showed me that John was still at the desk, but he had his head down, his eyes focused on the computer screen.

Tiptoeing across the tile floor, I'd made it to the bottom of the stairs before he stopped me.

"Ms. Lorcan! Are you all right? We did a head count after the earthquake and we couldn't find you. We had the police here and everything." I cringed as he spoke, feeling guilty, like a teenager caught sneaking out at night. But he said nothing about the five-foot-long snake across my shoulders.

I looked over at him. "I'm sorry. I didn't think. I just went for a walk to calm my nerves. The forest is peaceful, you know."

He nodded and gave me an understanding smile. "Of course, I feel the same way. But if there's another quake, do let us know if you plan on leaving the premises."

"Of course, I'm sorry for the trouble." I ran up the stairs, zipping past the first and second landing and finding myself on the third floor in a matter of seconds.

Cora chuckled in her makeshift hammock.

"Now you begin to see what it means to be quickened."

"What's happened to me? I mean, am I like an X-Men now? Or Superman?" I asked as I stepped through the threshold to my room and leaned against the door. If I had all this strength and speed, why couldn't I save Ashling?

"Quickening wakens the fae blood you carry as Luke pointed out. Because you are a half breed, you never would have been able to tap into your full powers without help. Now you are just as fast, strong and powerful as any full blooded Tuatha or Fomorii. You'll need training to reach your potential, of course, but for now, trust your instincts, Quinn, they will guide you. Believe in yourself, my girl."

A scent reached my nose and I breathed deeply. Rotting leaves and mold. I wrinkled my face up and sneezed. "That is awful."

She let out a low hiss. "It is the stink of a dead Fomorii. What have you been doing?" Cora said, slithering onto the king-size bed and stretching out to her full length.

I cringed. I'd conveniently forgotten about that little detail. I opened several windows to air the smell out. "I'll tell you over breakfast. But basically, I have the arms of a Fomorii in my closet."

I left Cora there while I ordered breakfast, showered, dressed and re-braided my hair.

The food, a full plate of waffles, toast, eggs, bacon and an extra-large hot chocolate. Every bite went in and Cora watched with what could only be approval in her eyes. "You burn the calories faster when you use your strength. Get used to eating more."

"Fine by me," I mumbled around a piece of bacon.

With the last of the food gone, it was time to get down to business.

We had to get moving and I had a thought that might bring the barrier down.

"My blade, my knife is special, isn't it?" I held it up for Cora to see the knife my grandpa had given me.

"It is special, that is true."

I rolled the handle across my palm. "It hurt the Fomorii that were in the water. And Grandpa gave it to me when he knew I was going diving because of the monsters which makes me think that maybe it's more than just special, that maybe it's magic. Is that true?" I stared hard at her, but it's hard to read a snake's facial expressions.

She didn't answer me, and I grimaced.

"Okay, fine. Just tell me one thing—is it strong enough, *special* enough, to break through that barrier?" I asked, leaning over the bed, my knife held between both hands.

Cora took a deep breath and wound herself around the knife, deftly taking it from me. Her tongue flicked out and tasted the steel. "With the right elements, yes, the blade could *possibly* cut through it. But I do not know that you can find those right elements."

I let out a sigh of relief. I knew I'd been right to trust Cora. "Then let's go!" Time was ticking away, I had sixteen hours to get to Ashling and Mom away from the Fomorii.

"It won't go through the thick part of the barrier, Quinn, no matter how strong you are now. The *right* elements must be present. You must be one of the Fomorii to travel through the barrier. If you could convince one of them to take you without harming you the knife might make the difference. . ."

My head drooped, excitement dulling. "We already know that won't happen." Luke had made it clear he wasn't going to help me through the barrier, and I had no doubt that Bres would be on Luke's side.

Cora unravelled herself from the knife. "No, it won't. I know of none who carry enough Fomorii blood to take your hand and walk you through the barrier."

I sat back on my heels; despair once more rising within me. The smell of rotted leaves assaulted my nose again. I jumped up, ran to the closet and flung the door open, gagging at the smell that enveloped me.

I pulled the black garbage bag out and held it up. I really, really did not want to open this.

Making a face, I took a shallow breath and asked, "So, does the Fomorii have to be alive to make walking though the barrier possible?"

12

Gagging and heaving, I opened the black plastic bag and poured the contents of what remained of the Fomorii's two arms into the tub. This was the only Fomorii that wasn't going to fight me again, and maybe I could use what was left of it to help me cross the barrier and get to Ashling.

One step at a time. I gagged hard as another waft of the rotting bits rolled past my nose.

The flesh was decomposing at an alarming rate, hell even the bones were barely more than mush. Damn, I'd been hoping to take one and just shove my way through the barrier. But there was still a lot of blood, even if most of it pooled in the bottom of the black garbage bag. Maybe I could still use it? I poured it into the tub with the arms, doing my best not to splash the horrid stuff about.

God, the housekeepers were going to hate me when I left.

"How did this happen again?" Cora asked, her blue scales flashing as she zipped across the floor and peeked over the side of the tub.

"It was last night. My power rose and I saw Ashling in the mirror, and then a Fomorii came through her cell door and attacked me. The mirror shattered and the arms fell off on my side of the mirror," I said as I pulled the neck of my T-shirt up over my nose and breathed through it. It wasn't much of a filter, but it was better than nothing at all.

"This might just work," she muttered. "Things happen for a reason, and you have the means to make this work." Her tail flicked around and she pointed with it to my knife and then to the pool of now black, rank blood in the bottom of the tub. "Dip your knife in the blood." I did as she said, gingerly putting the blade all the way in. Steam rose and the blood bubbled, the boiling action only intensifying the smell. I gagged and nearly dropped my knife.

"Don't go soft on me now. You've got worse

than this to face yet if you want to save them both," Cora said.

I shuddered. "I don't mind facing it. It's the smell I don't like."

As I drew the blade out the black blood seemed to absorb into it. I held it up to the light, twisting it every which way, noting the edge was no longer shining. "It's dulled the knife."

Cora grunted. "The blade is not dulled, only stained. Now your clothes."

I looked down at her. "Now my clothes what?" Again, she flicked the tip of her tail at the tub. She had to be kidding me. I stared at the tub, then looked at Cora. "Are you sure? Like really, really sure?" I asked.

She bobbed her head. "Yes. And if I thought you could stomach it; I'd have you drink some of it down. The more Fomorii blood on and *in* you, the better chance you'll have to not only cross that barrier, but to get to the Fomorii stronghold unnoticed."

Stripping down, I tossed my white shirt and light-colored jeans into the foul mess. They soaked the fluid right up and the smell lessened considerably. The white shirt was now a deep gray with flecks of red and black and the jeans looked as if someone had taken a can of rust colored spray paint to them. I pulled them out and held them up. They were perfectly dry.

"That is seriously freaky." I turned them around a few times. "This magic shit is weird, Cora."

"Put them on, Quinn. And then it is time for you to go," she said, slithering out of the bathroom and back up onto the king-sized bed where she coiled herself up into a tight bundle.

With a grimace, I pulled the shirt out and slipped it on, holding my breath as it passed over my face. Using my vanilla-scented body spray I made the attempt to improve the clothes, but it was no use. They smelled now like vanilla blended with a hint of rotting limbs and sea water—not really any better.

"You won't be coming with me?" I asked, stepping back into the bedroom. Already the fear began to build in my heart. I believed I could get through the barrier, that this was my chance. I just wasn't entirely sure what I would do once that happened. I still had to face the water, I had to get a boat and a dive suit, and a spear gun.

But if I couldn't make myself get into the water to save Ashling when I thought she was drowning, how the hell was I supposed to get into the water when I couldn't even see her?

Cora's voice brought me back to the present. "No, I will only be a hindrance to you as my blood will not let me pass the barrier. Luke was right. I am old and the battles are too much for me." She yawned. "Likely, I would fall asleep at an inopportune moment, leaving you to fend for yourself." She slid underneath one of the pillows, her voice muffled. "Try not to get killed. I rather like you."

Tucking the knife into my back pocket, I stood and took a deep breath, then gave a low gag. Damn it, this was rough on a tender stomach. That deep breath had not been a good idea.

Time was ticking, which meant if this was going to work, I had to get moving.

"Only one way to find out," I strapped my knife back into its neoprene sheath and grabbed my swimsuit. I could put it on later, after I got through the barrier. Down the stairs I went, passing the hotel front desk, making sure I didn't move too fast.

John wasn't there at the desk, but a woman with short red hair smiled and gave me a nod as I passed. I gave her a quick nod in return, and the spit in my mouth dried up. Her smile froze me to the spot. Her teeth were sharp, serrated, and filled her entire mouth as her grin stretched literally from ear to ear.

Call me crazy, but I didn't think she was human.

"Hello, Quinn," she said in a deep, raspy voice. "I've been hearing about you, and I just had to see for myself if'n you were the real deal-e-o. Why do you be smelling like one of my kin?"

Before she could so much as stand up, I bolted for the front door, my newfound speed lending me the edge I needed to get the hell out of there. She let out a shriek. A quick glance behind me showed she was in full pursuit.

Though she started out looking vaguely human that was obviously some sort of glamor. She ran like a dog on all fours, hunched over at the back, gills on the side of her neck flapping as her uniform seemed to absorb into her body leaving only the gray-black skin of a Fomorii. Shit, this was the last thing I needed when I was about to try and break through the barrier.

Leaping over benches and dodging people, I wondered why they weren't screaming and freaking out at this large monster running through their midst behind me. Of course, they couldn't see her. They couldn't see the Fomorii any more than the young couple had been able to hear Cora. They were just humans without a drop of fae blood in them.

Then I realized they weren't looking at me either.

The humans didn't see me when I was running flat out, using my newfound speed to avoid my monster pursuer.

Out of the forest I burst and into a parking lot where I slid across the hood of a car, landed on the other side and in a few strides was back in the forest and on the boardwalk.

She was a full blooded Fomorii . . .could I lead her to the barrier? An image of me bodily tackling the woman as we fell through the barrier seemed all too plausible. I just had to get us there.

Pumping my arms, I all but flew down the walkway with the Fomorii woman close behind. Her heavy, wet breath came out in sharp bursts, growling and snarling as she gave chase. She seemed further away than she truly was because several times her claws reached out and snagged at my jeans, nearly toppling me.

When I was almost to the barrier she slowed, the sounds of her breathing easing off.

"Oh no, you won't fool me into taking you across," she said, laughter bubbling out of her. I skidded to a stop, the barrier still ten feet away. Facing her, I pulled out my knife. She continued to laugh, louder and louder, the birds going silent around us as her mirth filled the air.

"That? You're going to fight me with a steak knife?" She snorted and put her head down, cracking her neck from side to side, her gills flipping open and closed. "You're going to die, Tuatha. And then I'm going to feast on your flesh."

My breathing quickened and my hand tightened on the bone handle. "You're right, I will die. But not today." I flipped the blade in my hand, caught the tip and threw it at her—all in less time than it took to blink.

Like watching a slow-motion screen shot, the knife spun through the air and landed with a solid thunk in the middle of her forehead, splitting open her single, protruding eye. A burst of fluid sprayed outward, covering the foliage, and the Fomorii dropped to the mossy forest floor without a single sound.

I ran toward her, but the body was sinking into the ground fast, the moss covering her. I bent and yanked my knife out of her eye as the last of her was swallowed by the plant life. The blade came out with a sick popping sound that released another spray of fluid. Stumbling backward, a strong set of hands gripped my arms.

I spun and struck out with the knife blindly. Damn it, she had a friend with her?

Bres stood a few feet back, his hands in the air. "Easy, Quinn."

I stalked over to him.

He wrinkled his nose. "It smells like you've been playing with the enemy," Bres said, his voice teasing. Another time I wouldn't have cared. But the blood was still flowing hot from the chase and the quick fight with the Fomorii woman. I reacted without really thinking, snapping my fist out and punching him in the side of the jaw. He stumbled away from me with a curse, his hand to his face and his violet eyes flashing.

"What the hell is wrong with you?" he growled.

"You know, if you'd just been doing your job, I wouldn't have had to face that Fomorii on my own. And where the hell were you when I really needed to be protected?" I asked, feeling my anger rise. Far better than the fear that had been coursing through me.

So much fear, so much I couldn't control, and I hated both of those things.

"You did fine on your own, Quinn, though Luke should have been here to help. I only just be relieving him of his watch," Bres said.

I tried another route, still angry and not willing to give up on my anger just yet. "If you are truly on my side, why don't you help me across the barrier? You do have Fomorii blood in you if I remember correctly. You are Balor's son, aren't you?"

"Unfortunately, yes, I am." He stared at me and I could see him trying to figure out who'd told me. He let out a snort. "No matter how you be baiting me, Quinn, I won't take you across the barrier," he said, rubbing his jaw. "Though I would like to see you give me father a cuff like that."

I scowled at him, angry that he wouldn't help me.

"How do you be enjoying your integration into the world of the Tuatha and Fomorii? Hmm. Do you like the sea monsters and the powers that be wanting to control your life?" He bent to get a closer look at me, the proximity of those violet eyes reminding me fiercely of his father's. "You've been quickened from what Luke said. You understand what that means?"

I nodded.

He smiled down at me, white teeth flashing. "How do it feel to be one of the elite?" He was too close, the intensity of his eyes too much, and I pulled away, noting how those very eyes narrowed, and his lips tightened.

"It's fine," I said, not wanting to look him in the eyes.

Bres stepped close to me, his body very close, very claustrophobic. "If you are going to be angry at anyone, I think it should be Luke. He's the one that be keeping secrets from you, not me."

I lifted my eyes. "What do you mean?"

He smiled. "I'm not allowed to tell you, Quinn. They be Luke's secrets. I just do as I'm told like a good soldier." He stepped back and bowed toward me, his eyes laughing at me though his lips remained still.

"Then what good are you to me?" I asked, poking him in the chest.

"Command me, oh, great one, leader of the armies, battle queen of the Tuatha. Tell me what you will and let me, the lowly Fomorii half-blood, grovel to do your will." He winked, but I refused to be pulled into his game.

I put my hand on my hips. "Are you here to help me or are you just here to get in my way?"

"You can't be going after her. It's too dangerous and you mean too much to the Tuatha. They will never risk you for her," he said, his tone changing from mirth to somber in a split second.

"She's my sister. I won't leave her there. And they have my mother too," I said. He frowned and I frowned back at him, though I noted he was having far too much fun at my expense.

"I won't let you go, Quinn. It's me job to protect you. Come, we have to leave now." He reached out and grabbed my hand, all but yanking me off my feet.

"Hey!" I yelped and snatched my hand back from him. What was it with these men anyway? They seemed to be stuck in the past when a woman could be bullied and pushed into doing what the men wanted.

I turned my back to him and strode the last ten feet to the barrier. Bres was muttering behind me but I ignored him, ignored the fear that rose when I thought of what came after the barrier came down. I gritted my teeth. With or without his help I was going to get Ashling back.

Right now.

13

I strode the last ten feet to where I knew the barrier stood between me and getting to Ashling.

Lifting the knife with both hands, I drove it forward with all my newfound strength. The blade biting deeply into the barrier.

The shockwave of the weapon hitting such a hard surface ricocheted up my arm and rattled my teeth, but I hung on for all I was worth. The shaking continued and I realized it was another earthquake, one that had me hanging from the blade, my body swinging like a pendulum, until both I and the knife were thrown clear of the barrier.

Timing was everything I suppose, and my timing was shit apparently.

I hit the ground hard, the wind rushing out of me in a single whoosh. Flat on my back I stared up at the underside of the tree branches. Damn it.

Bres started to laugh and that only spurred me onward. I stood, dusted my clothes off and tried again. And again, and again. Each time, the blade would bite into the barrier and each time the barrier forced the blade out. I leaned into it with all I had, pressing my Fomorii blood-soaked clothing against the barrier too, but nothing helped. Tears of frustration and anger built, and it took all I had not to scream at the barrier.

"Ah, give it up, Quinn. I could have told you that it wouldn't work," Bres said, laughter filling his voice.

Lying on the ground for the fourth time, I fought with the tears that threatened to spill over. I had been so sure it *would* work. Cora had been sure it would work. No, that was wrong, she'd said possibly. I pushed to my feet and stared at the spot where my knife had entered the barrier and couldn't see anything. I ran my fingers over the barrier, there wasn't a single crack I could feel—

not even a small depression. I hadn't done a thing to it.

Bres came to stand beside me. "You aren't going to get in there, Quinn. So, stop trying."

I rubbed my arm where I'd landed on it wrong. The pain was already fading, which was good—yeah for fast healing. I shook my head at Bres. "I'm not giving up on her. I refuse to. And she wouldn't give up on me, not for anything."

He stared down at me and the air seemed to thicken between us. Bres was far too much like his father for my comfort. I pulled away from him, again seeing hurt in his eyes before he hid it with a laugh. "You pull away as if I be having a disease. Being a Fomorii isn't contagious."

My face heated and I pushed myself away from him. "That's not why I pulled away." I stood and dusted my clothes off.

He chuckled. "No? Then what is it, my stunning good looks that you be too afraid you might fall for me instead of wee Luke?"

I snorted and decided to tell him the truth. No point in trying to spare his feelings seeing as he seemed bound and determined to laugh at me. "You look like your father and he scared me."

There was a beat of silence before Bres

grabbed my upper arm and started to drag me toward the hotel. "Hey, let me go!" I yelped.

"You are not going anywhere near that barrier again. I'm taking you back to the hotel and then Luke be getting your flight out of here today. No more games, Quinn. You be done here." he said, seemingly unconcerned with the fact that he was dragging me along. His jaw twitched repeatedly, and I realized that I must have hit a sensitive spot when I'd compared him to his father. Too late to take it back now.

"You can't do this!" I screeched, flinging my entire body away from him. Dark power—so like Balor's—wrapped itself around me, stopping my attempts to free myself. Dark like the night and the moon. Bres stared down at me, "Stop being a ninny. Unlike my father, I be trying to keep you alive." That didn't make me feel a whole lot better and since I couldn't free myself, I tried a new tactic. One I was pretty sure would work.

"Luke!"

An instant later, Luke was standing in front of us, his eyes narrowed and his long sword once more bared to the world.

"Oh, come now, Luke, you know she's safe with me. I would never hurt her," Bres said. "She's being a spoiled brat for not getting her way, so she tattled on me to you." He gave my arm a shake as if to make a point.

"I don't want to go with him, Luke," I said. "And I'm not particularly keen on being dragged about."

Luke looked torn as his eyes went between me and Bres. "Let her go. We're supposed to protect her, not control her."

Bres's hand tightened on my arm. "And when she's killed because you want her so much, you won't do the right thing? What then? You know she shouldn't be anywhere near this barrier, and yet you let her roam free. She should be locked in that damn room until we get this sorted out and get the flight settled."

Luke's jaw tightened and he lowered the sword. "I will escort her to her room then while you make the necessary arrangements."

"No!" I yelled as Bres handed me off to Luke like a naughty kid being sent to my room, still partially bound up with his darker power.

I was nearly twenty-three, not a child, and this was ridiculous!

At the front desk, John stood quietly while Bres spoke with him. "John! Don't help them!" I yelled. But the manager didn't even notice as I was dragged up the stairs, kicking and screaming as much as I was able to against the bond Bres had wrapped around me.

Luke opened the door and all but threw me inside. "That's enough, Quinn. We are doing what we can to save you sister."

I drew a shuddering breath and wobbled my way to the pine desk. "What?"

"The council is negotiating with the Fomorii right now. They believe they can get Ashling back, but . . ."

My head dropped. "Not my mother."

"I'm sorry. You are the priority. Ashling they will try to save because she means so much to you. Your mother is not even half Tuatha. She is just another human with a dash of fae blood. It isn't enough to risk Tuatha lives to save her," he said, his eyes softening.

Cora slithered out from under the pillows. "The boys got in your way again, didn't they?"

"Yes," I snapped.

"No." Luke said. "Our job is to keep her safe."

She laughed.

"This isn't a game, Cora," I slumped into a chair. "Lives are at stake and they don't really give a shit about my sister or my mom."

Wriggling into a loose bundle of coils she bobbed her head. "Lives are always at stake, Quinn. You just have to be strong enough to know when they can be saved, and when they can't. You have to know when to cut your losses, my girl."

The silence grew heavy in the room and I was about to speak and say that I was not going to cut any damn losses when there was a knock at the door.

Luke motioned for me to stay where I was as he opened it. Of course, it was just Bres. He had a basket full of fruits, cheese and crackers, cookies, pastries and two jars of champagne along with a lovely bouquet of wildflowers. I wrinkled my nose at the strong smell.

Bres put the basket on the table and popped a couple cherries into his mouth. "Eat up, we have a long flight back to Oiland."

Frowning, I tried to decipher his accent. What was that? Where were we going?

I was reaching for an apple when the translation twigged. I froze. "What? Ireland?" I felt the blood drain from my face. The room seemed to swirl and jump, and I realized that it was another earthquake. It was over quickly. Probably just an aftershock.

Ireland. About as far from Ashling as I could be taken.

"Ireland. Whether you're ready or not, you need the council to back you as you step into your new role. They won't leave Tara, the seat of their power. We have to take you to them," Luke said as he mimicked Bres and took a handful of grapes and dropped them his mouth.

I lowered myself into a chair, shock making me quiet, as the conversation went on around me.

"Did you get the helicopter?" Luke asked.

"Yes, it'll be here in less than half a' hour. The pilot knows we need to be at the Comox airport for our connecting flight. We'll be flying out from there and hopscotch our way across the continent. We be heading for Dublin by way of Chicago tomorrow morning."

My ears shut down as I contemplated my options few as they were. They wanted me to leave, to just to run away and protect myself while I left Ashling, and my mom, with the Fomorii. If I was this chosen person they believed me to be, why weren't they listening to me? Could I command them to do what I told them to?

"No, you couldn't." Cora slithered over to me and

I picked her up and set her in my lap. Again, she seemed to read my mind, not that I minded in that instance. But maybe I could make it work for me?

The Fomorii that had bit me while I'd been in the water had spoken directly to my mind. I needed to talk to Cora without the boys listening in. It wouldn't hurt to try. If nothing happened, no one would even know that I'd made the effort. I concentrated just on Cora, blocking out any thought of the two men in the room.

IF I TALK IN MY HEAD LIKE THIS, CAN YOU HEAR ME? I asked her.

She gave a shiver. *Not so loud. But yes, I can hear you.*

I thought for a minute. *Do you think the council is truly trying to get Ashling out? Or are they just telling me what I want to hear?*

Cora flicked her tongue in and out several time before answering. *No, they won't be trying to get Ashling out. There are too many other lives at stake to bother with one little girl that they believe has no value, even if it isn't true.*

My jaw tightened. I needed a plan. A good one that the boys couldn't wreck. *Cora, I need to get through that barrier. How can I do that when I can't get away from Luke and Bres?* I tried not to think about the water aspect. One step at a time.

She went very still, and for a moment, I thought she hadn't heard me. *Perhaps I can help you there, but you must trust me completely.*

I gave her a subtle nod. *Yes, I trust you, Cora. What do you need me to do?*

I fed her a piece of my apple while she answered. *The last such great barrier was flat but tall, hundreds of feet tall. To make a dome would require far too much energy, more than Balor could have if he pulled on all of the Fomorian's within his kingdom.*

What does that have to do with anything? How would he have made the barrier?

Cora shifted her body, getting more comfortable before answering. *He would have drawn on the life forces of the Fomorii he rules. For a barrier this size, many of them would have lost their lives to give him this protection.*

I shuddered and shook off the magic lesson.

You must be prepared to face your fear of the water. For when the moment comes that I help you breach the barrier, there will be no turning back. Luke will do all he can to stop you. He will try to protect you with everything he has because he believes with all his heart that you are destined to be his, not that he loves you. Do you understand?

I nodded and gave her a small, tight smile. I did understand, and I felt the same way. I was drawn to Luke, but I doubted the truthfulness of that feeling. His power was seductive, and the idea of fate bringing us together was romantic, but none of that was love.

The secondary part, the very thought of the water over my head as I swam down through the depths to find my family. Of the monsters that would drag me to my death as I was eaten alive—all but stilled my heart with fear.

For Ashling and Mom, I would do all I could, I would try with all I had. I had to make every effort to fight my way to them, to free them from Balor and the Fomorii. Though I didn't say it to Cora, my heart whispered the truth of it to me, as sweat began to pool in the hollow of my back.

I didn't think I could do it.

14

There was a helicopter pad not far from the Wickaninnish hotel and that was where the boys hustled me a short fifteen minutes later.

Fifteen minutes after that, right on time, the helicopter picked us up and we were airborne within moments. I fidgeted with the wildflowers I gripped tight in my hands, waiting on Cora's cue. She sat in Bres's lap, his face a mask of concentration, occasionally nodding, then frowning. They were speaking, of that I was sure, and with the looks Bres kept sending my way I had no doubt of the subject matter upon which they were discussing.

I hadn't bothered to change out of my Fomorii

blood-soaked clothes, though I had kept my knife strapped on. I thought the time to make a go of tackling the barrier would have come by now and each second that it took before she spoke the go word—snakeskin—I grew more agitated.

"Luke, you should fly us over the water where Quinn's sister was taken. Let her say goodbye properly, for we both know the council and how they work," Cora said. How she was heard over the wind and the rotors I have no idea.

Luke's eyes softened and he nodded, tapping the pilot on the shoulder and directing him to the surfing area. My mouth was suddenly dry. What the hell was Cora thinking? Surely not . . .

"How high up are we?" I asked into the headset, my voice shaking. I didn't like heights any more than I liked water.

The pilot answered. "About two hundred feet, give or take. You afraid of heights?"

I tried to build up some spit to answer him but had to settle for a nod. Bres came to stand beside me and Luke, his eyes narrowed as he stared down at me. Did he suspect that Cora and I had a plan? Sweet heaven above, I wished she'd given me an inkling to the idea that she'd had. All she'd said was 'take the flowers, you'll need them to cover your move'.

We banked to the left and soon we were hovering over the spot where Ashling had been taken. I played with the bouquet. "Throw those flowers out to your sister," Cora said, her eyes unfathomable. "She would like that, I think, a last goodbye. Luke, open the door for her."

Please tell me you don't want me to jump. She didn't answer, just flicked her tongue out, tasting the air.

Luke pulled the door open and a blast of air swirled in. A gasp escaped me, and I found myself clutching both Luke and Bres, the flowers scrunched up in one hand. I turned and caught Cora's eye as she lay coiled on the bench seat. She nodded. *You are doing the right thing, Quinn. Your sister needs you. When the time comes, jump. Your body can handle the impact now that you've been quickened. You won't run out of air. You are Tuatha de Daanan. Swim to the bottom of the ocean—there you will find the Fomorii kingdom, and in it, your mother and sister. Save them.*

I gave a tight nod, not even trusting the voice I could project mentally. It might have been the right thing to do, but that didn't mean I was going to be able to do it.

Luke held his hand out to me, and I gripped his fingers, my knuckles turning white and he grimaced. "I won't let you fall, Quinn," he said.

I tried to swallow, couldn't, and felt a gag coming on. Two hundred feet up was no small thing and Cora wanted me to jump? She was right, I knew she was, but could I do it?

Rational Quinn was not on board with this idea.

"Here, I'll hold her. You make sure the pilot holds this be-damned contraption steady," Bres said, peeling my hands out of Luke's. Bres's hand settled in the small of my back and I found my fingers intertwined with his. He gave me a wink. Oh crap, he knew. This wasn't going to work. A spurt of relief flushed through me, followed closely by shame. Tears formed in my eyes.

Luke turned away, went to put a hand on the pilot.

Bres leaned into me, his mouth against my ear. "I know what you're doing, Quinn. Cora filled me in."

I stared up at him and his eyes twinkled down at me. "Now that I understand better, I think you are doing the right thing. And, to prove it, I'm coming with you."

"SNAKESKIN." Cora yelled over the rushing wind. Bres gave me a jerk. I gripped the edge of the helicopter, my fingers biting into the metal. I loved my family, but I couldn't do this—I just couldn't.

"Luke!" I screamed, knowing he would save me from this. He would stop this madness.

I was a coward and I hated it.

Luke spun in time to see me wrestling with Bres as he peeled my hands out of their death grip. "Time to go meet your destiny, Quinn," Bres said.

My last finger slid off the cold metal. Luke jumped toward us and Cora struck, her body coiling around Luke's legs and dropping him to the corrugated floor with a clang.

"Bres, what are you doing?" Luke yelled.

Bres saluted Luke. "I be changing the world, Luke. Changing destiny."

I struggled in his hands, jerking my body left and right, the helicopter dancing under the lurches of our combined weight.

"You guys settle down back there. I can't keep her straight!" the pilot shouted back at us, totally unaware of what was going on.

With a final yank, Bres pulled me to his chest,

his arms snaking around me and holding me tight to him. "Hang on" was all he said before he jumped off the edge, taking me with him

Behind me, Luke screamed my name, and then there was only the rush of air as it filled my ears. The helicopter veered away from us and for a brief moment it felt as if I was floating. Time slowed as I stared out at the Pacific Ocean. Maybe this wouldn't be so bad. I glanced at Bres, his violet eyes full of laughter and sorrow intermingled. Then I looked down.

The ocean rushed toward us. Bres tipped us into a diving position. Facing the water, he yanked our hands above our heads, my body still pressed tightly against him. "Whatever you do, don't let go of me," he said as we *impossibly* picked up speed.

Fear filled me up and already I found myself pulling back, trying to somehow stop our headlong rush into the waves below which of course was a ludicrous thought. The waves were right there, I took a single breath—then my fingers split the water and we were submerged, our momentum driving us deep.

As the speed began to slow, I started to fight, memories and panic stripping me of any cohesive thought. I had to get out of the water. Now.

I spun and kicked hard; all my muscles focused on one task. Getting the hell out of the water and back to dry land as fast as possible.

But Bres wasn't about to let me go. He kept a hand clamped around my waist and started to swim downward, the fight between us took us into cold, dark waters. Very quickly the light from the surface was lost, and we were swimming blindly in the dark. With each stroke he took, I tried to reach back to the surface, praying he would tire, and I could get away. His power swirled out around me again, binding my limbs so I could no longer fight him.

Panic clawed at me. Though Cora had said I didn't need to worry about holding my breath, I wanted to breathe. I didn't know how much longer I could hold my breath and the darkness was disorienting me, the pressure on my eardrums intensifying. Something circled around my ankles.

I fought like a wild animal, every memory of the shark attack hitting me at once, my body and mind fighting to stay alive.

A light bloomed and Bres held a globe of fire—how it managed to stay lit in the water, I didn't know, but it showed my attacker clearly. A Fomorii clung to my leg, its mouth open and ready to chomp down on my calf.

Again. I was going to get another set of shark teeth in my leg.

Bres's voice filled my mind—and, obviously, the mind of the Fomorii as well since it shrank away from him, releasing my leg. *Do not make that mistake. I am taking her to Balor. He will decide what to do with her.*

Maybe I wasn't supposed to hear that? Was Bres a traitor? The Tuatha should have known though. He was Balor's son. How could he be trusted? Maybe he was trying to fool the Fomorii? But then why hadn't he just helped me through the barrier?

Two Fomorii snaked toward us, their bodies undulating through the black water, mouths open, claws outstretched.

Bres swam toward them. His attention wavered and with it the bindings on me suddenly gave way. I jerked out of his arms.

With everything I had, I swam upward—away from Bres, away from the Fomorii. My heart cried out at the coward I was, that I didn't have it in me to save Ashling, no matter how I said I wanted to. I would plead for her with the council. Surely, they had the strength to bring her back.

Grab her. The command was simple—Bres giving orders to his Fomorii brethren. Hands and claws gripped each of my limbs and they towed me back to the depths.

With the Fomorii hanging off me and Bres leading the way, I was dragged into the ocean's darkest hollows, even though I fought them every second. Fear dug at me, sharper than the Fomorii clawed hands, sharper than my knife. The panic so bad that at one point I passed out, floating in a world of nothing, blissfully unaware for a period of time.

I don't know how long we went downward, or when I came to. I only knew that the pressure on my ears increased with each second. The darkness pressed in heavy on us and the small globe that Bres held afloat was our only guiding light —literally.

Leave her to me. Bres commanded and the Fomorii obeyed. I was exhausted from fighting the Fomorii and Bres, my limbs limp with the struggle. The fear that had ridden me so hard was only a bare flicker in my belly now. Bres grabbed my hand and dragged me forward. I kicked, helping us along. Bres turned surprised eyes my way. I tipped my face away from his. I was here now, there was no going back.

I would do all I could to free Ashling and Mom now that I was past the worst of the cowardice and fear.

I reached to take another stroke and my hand broke the surface of the water, my head popping out right behind. Though I didn't seem to need to breathe while under water, no matter the length of time, I still found myself gasping for air now that I *could* breathe. The world swayed and this time it was no earthquake. Lightheaded from holding my breath so long, I struggled to pull myself to the edge of the cavern we appeared to be in.

Bres tread water beside me and I took a deep breath and asked, "How long have you been playing both sides?"

I stared at him, my temper rising even more as he answered in clipped tones.

"Perhaps you should think twice before speaking. Maybe, just maybe, we should try to get in, find Ashling and your mom, and escape with as few Fomorii knowing we be here as possible. Hmm?"

He hoisted himself out of the water, bent and

pulled me up, holding me so that my feet dangled in the air and my face was right in his.

"You aren't on my side." I said.

"I *am* on your side. Remember that you wanted to be here, that you said you trusted Cora. She thought this was best for you and I agreed after she explained a few things to me," His eyes flashed with temper. He let go of me unceremoniously and I hit the ground hard, my feet stinging with the impact.

My legs were wobbly, but they would hold me up. I took a few steps away from him and wrung out my hair, squeezing as much water as I could from my curls and clothes.

"Why are you helping? What did Cora say to you?" I wished it was Luke, not Bres with the disturbing eyes and looks so like his father that stood across from me, helping me. Luke because he was easier on me, because he would be soft on me.

Bres scrubbed his fingers though his dark hair. "Look, you don't have the strength yet to save your family without help. Plus, if we get caught, I may be able to talk us out of it. I am the son of Balor, remember?" He held his hand up and the glowing ball of blue fire appeared over his palm. "Cora convinced me that this be a part of your destiny, that you must be here now, that you must be allowed to follow your heart no matter where it takes you. But she was concerned your fears would hold you back and that you would need help to get this far. And by the way, she was not wrong."

I flushed, embarrassment coursing through me. I'd fought to get back to the surface basically until I'd passed out. Cora and Bres were right. I couldn't have come this far on my own, my fears crippling my ability to move forward. Even if I'd found my own way through the barrier, I doubted if I could have made myself go in the water. No, no doubt—I knew I wouldn't have been able to go in the water.

I swallowed my pride. "Thank you. You're right, I wouldn't have got this far without your help. Even though I . . .I wanted to."

He blew out a big breath. "You are welcome. Now, let's get moving."

A large boom sounded deep within the cave and the underwater cavern we'd just swam out of sealed off, a cap of rock sliding over the opening. Bres stared at me. "We'll be lucky if we survive it."

I frowned, my heart picking up speed. "Survive what?

He laughed at me and walked away as I hurried to catch up to him. He swept an arm out in front of us, "We're in the labyrinth of the Fomorii, Quinn. It's designed to keep people out and trap those who are not worthy. Those who enter uninvited are never seen again."

15

The labyrinth of the Fomorii, that I had to somehow navigate in order to find Ashling and my mom, was not particularly awe inspiring. More like it needed a serious make-over renovation.

The walls were lit from within which gave off a soft glowing illumination—enough to see by, though not well. The ground was wet and slippery with green and yellow algae, and it took a lot of concentration not to stumble with every step. On a closer inspection, it wasn't the walls that were glowing but the algae itself, a soft green glow that gave everything a fuzzy and indistinct quality.

What I was surprised about was that it didn't

smell terribly bad. To be fair, it didn't smell like much of anything at all. Not even the smell of the ocean which was expected.

Bres kept up a quiet running commentary as we navigated our way. "There be a number of challenges we could face. Fire, poison, temptations and, of course, the more twisted Fomorii are kept here as pets, the ones that be less human like. With each challenge we pass the next will be more difficult. I know of only one person who ever made it all the way through the labyrinth, and he was nearly dead when he crawled out. That made it easy for my da to kill him."

I didn't want to think about Balor right now, the feeling of his power weighing down on me. "Tell me about the Tuatha. How is it that they've hidden from the world all these years? And why?"

Bres shrugged and helped me over a pile of rubble where the roof had started to cave in. "Like anything with magic, there requires a certain amount of belief and faith to keep it alive. The Fomorii have flourished because the world has continued to produce monsters and darkness of varying kinds, which feeds their power. The Tuatha are, for the most part, full of light and compassion. That's still in the world, of course, but not to the extent that fear is. Luke, he used to go by a different name. Lugh."

He paused and I kept quiet as I could feel his indecision of what to tell me.

"He changed his name like so many of the fae did to fit in better. And of course, he has been a champion of the Tuatha for many years, waiting for his love to be born." That last was said with only a small amount of sarcasm.

We came to a T junction, our first decision. "Why are you being so up front with me now?" I asked. "Before, I could barely get you to say two words to me."

Bres laughed, took my hand and rolled it over, exposing my wrist. Very slowly, his eyes never leaving mine, he lowered his head and placed a kiss on the sensitive skin, his tongue trailing a pattern of fire over me. I jerked my hand away, a feeling of guilt following the flush of heat his tongue imbibed me with. It was Luke that I was supposed to be with, not Bres.

"*. . . her heart will remain pure, loving only the Shining One. . .*" He said softly.

That was part of the prophecy, so why did my body react to his touch?

And why the hell was he doing this? To prove a point?

He lifted his head and I blushed. There was no way he could miss the way my heart was hammering out of control. It seemed to me to be echoing between the walls.

"Prophecy or not, I don't think you even know what you truly want. Why not give you some options? As Cora suggested, you should be following your heart to your destiny, not what others 'spect of you." Bres gave me a long slow wink that stole the moisture from my mouth.

My clothing was suddenly too tight, and I had an insane desire to see if his kiss would steal away my senses the way Luke's did.

I let out a shuddering breath, quelling my suddenly raging hormones.

Rational Quinn said I was being distracted from what I needed to focus on which was getting Ashling out of this place.

I cleared my throat and rubbed at the wrist he'd kissed. "What about this training I'm supposed to get, how does that work?" If I just kept asking questions, maybe I could keep his mind occupied on other things. Safer, and far more mundane things. My heart was still beating wildly, a horse in a full-out gallop down a winding hillside. All from that one little kiss on the wrist. What would it be like if he put his lips to mine?

Holy shit, I'd probably burst into flames.

Forcing myself to look away from his violet eyes, I leaned my head into the junction and looked down one way and then the other. Both were dark, both held no hint as to what lay in their shadows.

He pointed to the left and I took the lead, determined to prove I wasn't a complete coward.

"Your training will come at the hands of the council. Until then, you'll fumble along, picking up tricks to use your abilities as you go. Many times, if you be put in a place of need, your abilities will manifest and you'll be able to use them on instinct," he said, the wavering patterns of his glowing bulb of fire dancing on the walls around us.

I thought about my Grandpa and how he'd taught me to fight, to tie knots, anything that could be used in a survival situation. Maybe I wasn't as useless as Bres and the others thought.

"How do you make that fire ball? Maybe I

could hold one too. It would give us more light," I said.

Bres opened his mouth to answer me but was interrupted by a low growl from a tunnel off to the left of us. The noise was followed swiftly by the scrabble of claws on the rock.

As far as I was concerned that made the decision for us. "Let's go!" I yelped; my eyes wide as I leaped forward.

"No, Quinn it's a trick!" Bres yelled after me, but it was too late. The darkness swallowed me completely, the dim light from the walls vanishing. I ran as fast as I dared with one hand on the wall and one hand out in front of me. Minutes passed before I slowed to listen. It was then that I realized Bres wasn't with me.

"Crap." I spun slowly, facing what I thought was the way I'd come. There was no noise, no heavy breathing of a monster about to chew me up and spit me out. Nothing. The sound of my own panting and the hammering of my heart in my ears was all that filled the silence I'd stupidly stuck myself with. One hand on the wall, I began to work my way back toward the start of the labyrinth. But after half an hour of walking in the dark, I knew I was stuck in some sort of merry-go-round. One that had no off switch.

Unable to even see my own hand, there was no way to even tell if there was an offshoot from the other side of the tunnel that I couldn't touch, the hall too wide to put a hand on either side. I put my back against the wall and slid down till my butt was on the cold rock floor. I needed to think this through, otherwise, without any effort on their part, the Fomorii had won on the first gambit. They would have bested me with the simplest of tricks. Not even a single monster for me to fight off —not that I was complaining about that.

Anger at myself and my stupid decision started to burn low in my gut. I couldn't let the Fomorii win but how was I supposed to find my way out of here? I needed something, some help, some light. Anything.

"Ashling," I whispered her name, my anger fading as sorrow filled me. Bres wouldn't go after her, neither would Luke or the council. She only had me to depend on and I sure was doing a bang-up job of rescuing her. I thumped my head back into the wall. I was an idiot. A coward and an idiot. If Cora hadn't made Bres grab me and jump I wouldn't even be this far.

Tears trickled down my cheeks in the darkness, the smell of stale seawater filling my nose. I didn't bother to wipe the tears away. There was no one to see them anyway. My cell phone was jabbing me from my back pocket. I pulled it out, but it was dead from being submerged. I wished I could just call Ashling the way I used to. Wait, maybe I could. . .

"All or nothing," I said, my voice echoing through the tunnels. I took a deep breath that exhaled past my lips in a shudder. I focused all my energy on her name.

ASHLING?

I waited for a minute then did a mental calling thingy again. There was nothing. Maybe we weren't close enough. Maybe I wasn't doing it right. A lot of maybes but if I could connect with anyone, it would be my sister. I stood and started to make my way down the tunnel again, always keeping a hand in front and a hand on the slimy wall, periodically calling out.

Why did Bres think this labyrinth was so bad? Sure, it was dark, which was totally disconcerting, but other than that original beastie, there had been nothing dangerous or even frightening. No traps, no fire-breathing dragons. My hand on the wall suddenly encountered empty space. I stopped, the breeze flowing toward me smelling like a BBQ. My mouth watered.

ASHLING?

Very distantly she replied, *I can hear you. Hurry, I'm here.*

She sounded like she was down the tunnel that brought me the smell of fire-roasted steaks. Suddenly ravenous, I found myself running down the side tunnel heading toward a small glimmer of light. Finally, a break!

The light grew, and by the time I could see clearly, I was stepping into a massive well-lit cavern with stalactites hanging above my head, the tips of them glowing bright like over amped halogens. In the center of the room, there was a table that would have easily seated thirty people, and it was completely covered with food. Twenty feet to the left of the table was a deep pit over which roasted an entire pig. To the right was a king-sized, four-poster bed draped in filmy gauze and covered in a pile of pillows and blankets.

I licked my lips and swallowed the rush of saliva that filled my mouth. I looked around the room. It was empty of anyone else. Where was Ashling?

I am here. The voice seemed to come from behind me.

I spun to see a hulking Fomorii hopping toward me. The creature only had a single leg with a wide flat foot, but it used its overlong arms to leverage itself across the ground, like a person on crutches. Dark blue skin mottled with open sores, greasy long hair looked like seaweed in dreadlocks, and it had the familiar open mouth full of teeth. It easily stood over twelve feet tall, far larger than any of the other Fomorii I'd encountered so far.

It started to laugh. "You were so easy to draw in, almost as easy as your man." It flicked one clawed hand toward the pit, and I stopped myself from turning to stare. Could Bres have been caught? No, I refused to believe it.

"That is not Bres and he's not my man," I said, forcing myself to believe it, nausea replacing the hunger I'd felt only moments before. "He knows this place. He wouldn't be caught by you."

The Fomorii snorted. "Bres, he doesn't know this place as he once did. Nor was he as safe as he believed himself to be."

I frowned at the beast as it settled itself in the long table, easily taking up the one side. It motioned for me join it.

"I get so little company, no one comes to the labyrinth any longer, certainly no one interesting. If you don't mind, before I kill you, I'd like to chat. Tell me, what is going on topside? Hmm?" The Fomorii reached for a platter of raw squid and poured the entire trencher into its gullet, teeth slicing and slashing at the squiggly snack.

I was not about to sit down and eat with this monster. I didn't think about it, I just turned on my super speed and ran. Sprinting toward the door, my heart sank. Bars slid downward to block my escape before I'd even taken three steps. If I was going to make it, the move I'd have to employ would make Indiana Jones proud.

The Fomorii roared as I drew close to the doorway, all this amped up quickening of my blood working in my favor. I *was* going to make it. A deep breath and I started to adjust my angle so I could slide under the lowering bars. This was going to be close.

A foot from the doorway the Fomorii grabbed me from behind, its oversized hand circling my body, its claws piercing my side. I screamed with sudden pain as my flesh popped like a grape skin. I called my knife to my hand and used it to slash at the fingers driving what felt like daggers into me.

The bars clanged behind me, but they were secondary to the fact that I was suddenly fighting for my life.

The Fomorii howled and reared its head back to strike with that great hulking mouth. There was no way I could defend myself from this. Bres was right. I had no idea what I was getting into. I was going to die in this labyrinth, leaving Ashling and Mom to fend for themselves against Balor.

In slow motion, I watched as the Fomorian's mouth descended then I turned my head, not wanting that gaping maw to be the last thing I saw. My eyes caught a glimmer of movement on the other side of the bars. Out of the darkness of the tunnel, through the bars, a long sword came hurtling toward us. I closed my eyes and felt the Fomorii jerk, its claws digging hard into my body. Turning my head, I saw the handle of the sword sticking out of the Fomorian's mouth, the steel tip out the back of its head, ending its bingeing spree along with its life.

Trapped in the Fomorian's hand with three claws still stuck deep inside of me, I fell to the ground with the monster, slumping onto my left side. There was a voice calling to me but there was something wrong. He sounded worried, scared even.

I tried to open my eyes, tried to see him, because if I was remembering right, he was worth looking at, though he bothered me a lot. I liked those violet eyes on him. But it was no use. I could no longer stay in the moment, the Fomorii had won.

16

The first thing I could feel as I came to were hands on my bare skin, rubbing something slick and minty smelling into it. That smell and the gentle pressure of hands eased some of the pain rolling through me.

A flash of memory climbed through me of the monstrous Fomorii tackling me to the ground, claws puncturing my body, the sword flying between the bars and Bres calling to me.

I lifted my nose to breathe deeply and a sharp pain in my side drew a groan from me. I slowly opened my eyes. A shirtless Bres, his hands covered in a clear, slick poultice, sat in front of me and the pain seemed to fade in the distance.

My eyes traveled over his sculpted torso following a tattoo that curled up his ribcage. Celtic designs I didn't understand and yet they drew me to them. Maybe it was the haze of pain that made me bold, or the feeling of being in a dream, but I reached out and slid my hand across his skin, tracing the pattern. Dark and dangerous, I knew that the meaning of them held the night and the moon and all that power. Of that, at least I was sure, though how I knew I couldn't tell. They were so familiar to me, like a long-forgotten memory. I felt like I should be able to understand what they meant. Bres's muscles tightened under my hand.

"Stop that." He said the words, but he didn't push me away.

"Where's your shirt?" I asked, my voice husky. "You should put it on."

"I used it to staunch the blood. Does it bother you?" His eyes were steady on mine.

"No, I guess not," I said, my hands still tracing the pattern of the tattoo. "I can almost read these. They are so familiar." Even though I was sure that I'd never seen them before.

His hand covered mine and the smell of mint grew stronger. "Quinn..." His voice was husky and again my eyes traveled over him. Low slung, snug pants allowed a great view of the muscling that drew my eyes downward, a perfect symmetry of strength and temptation.

I blinked and really realized that this was no dream. Mouth suddenly dry, I looked away and tried to draw my hand from his. My fingers slid through his easily and a tremble rippled through me, centering in my belly and spreading outward. I should not be here like this, not when I knew Luke was the one for me, that's what everyone was saying.

Wasn't he?

I cleared my throat. "Thank you. For saving me. You were right, I'm not going to make it on my own here."

Bres didn't say anything, just sat there in a perfect crouch as I tried to get my bearings. I was on the king-sized bed, pillows supporting every side of me. The table where the Fomorii had sat to eat was still there, as was the roasting pig—if that's what it actually was.

"Why were you mean to me when we first met?" I asked.

He stared at me, his eyebrows lifting high. "You really want to know?"

I nodded. "Yeah. I do."

He grimaced. "The prophecy says that you be meant for Luke. And since you seem to have bought into the whole pile of destiny crap they be feeding you, I didn't think you'd like me tempting you away from him. I wondered if I'd be able to without any real ability to Charm."

I laughed even as I flushed. "You, tempt me? Please. Just now? I was just, you know admiring your tattoo." I fumbled for the right words.

"Leading me on?" Bres offered, the corner of his lips turned up. Barely containing a smile.

I nodded, then winced. "Yes. Exactly. You are a Fomorii. I can't be with you. Don't want to anyway. I thought you were Luke for a minute there." Which was ridiculous of course, they were as different as night and day.

His eyes hardened reminding me very much that he was at one time with the Fomorii in every way, that he'd met Luke on the battlefield at some point. "Luke be half Fomorii, you know."

I nodded feeling the situation spiralling. I had to put distance between us. Had to before something happened. "Yes, but he doesn't act like it. You do."

"Do I? Hmm. Well, if one is going to be accused

of a crime, might as well commit it, don't you think?" he said, his eyes back to their devious twinkling that made me think he was laughing at me.

He lunged toward me and I fell backward onto the pillows, his body pressing mine into the soft bedding. Noses touching, I stared into his eyes, drowning in those violet depths and not minding one bit. My breath came in short sharp bursts. It must have been the wounds. Heat pooled in my belly, spreading through me. It must have been a low-grade infection from the claws. I would *not* feel this feeling and desire for Bres.

"What would you do if I claimed you as me own?" he whispered and my eyes widened, lips parting involuntarily.

"You can't do that. I'm not some trinket to claim," I said, trying to be tough, my words coming out breathy at best.

"No, that you aren't, me beautiful lady." He dropped his lips to mine and every other thought I had was washed away in the pleasure of his mouth, of the cold fire that thrilled through my body. My hands found their way to his hair, holding him tightly against me, demanding more. He let out a low groan against my mouth, left me there to kiss my neck, then along my jaw and back to my mouth.

"Tell me to stop, and I will," He murmured against my mouth.

But I couldn't, didn't want to because he didn't want me because of some prophecy. He just wanted me.

The kiss deepened and our two kinds of power swirled around us. I could feel it escalating, our energies twinning, tangling, becoming more together than they ever would be apart.

More even than I could be with Luke.

A weak cry escaped my lips as I tried to roll to one side, breaking off the kiss, the deep wounds feeling as if they were pulling me apart as I twisted. Not that I wanted to stop, but . . .Luke. Damn it.

Bres sat up, stared at me a moment, and I was glad to see his face looked as shell shocked as I felt.

"That wasn't supposed to happen," he muttered, got up and walked over to the table laden with food.

With his back to me, he picked at the feast. "You might as well get some sleep. We won't be leaving here until your wounds be at least partially knitted. Couple hours probably."

Okay so we were going with changing the subject and acting like that kiss hadn't happened. I could do that.

"How am I going to rescue anyone when I can't even keep myself in one piece?" I whispered. As I spoke the tears started. Maybe it was almost dying, maybe it was the emotions that he'd sparked. But the truth was I knew that I wasn't strong enough. Twice now he'd helped me to get just this far. "I'm no good to anyone. I can't be the one the prophecy speaks of. I can't even get over my fear of water! I can't even be faithful to the guy who my heart is supposed to only want!" So much for avoiding the subject of the kiss.

Bres turned and came back to the bed, sitting beside me. With great care, he pulled me into his arms. Tears poured out of me as all the fear, worry, guilt, shame, and anxiety over Ashling and my mom flowed along with the blood that trickled down my skin.

He held me through it all as I slowly pulled myself back together, my heart still aching, the guilt still reminding me of the things I had to make right. The emotions were, in a way, sharper than the claw wounds in my body—I knew they would take far longer to heal.

I laid my head against his chest and let his body warm me. Minutes passed and the proximity of his body and mine became a rather acute thing once more. The desire to touch him made me clench my fingers tight enough to drive my fingernails into my palms.

"Quinn." His voice startled me, and I jumped, the blanket that had been covering me slipping down, baring my shoulders and the tops of my breasts.

He stared down at me with a hunger so fierce I found it hard to breathe. Bres reached out, his hands sliding down my shoulders and arms then settling on my waist, the tingle from the poultice setting my skin to singing, the blanket pooling in my lap.

"You can't move yet," he said. "The wounds, they be needing time to heal. Traversing the labyrinth is dangerous enough without an injury."

"How long?" I asked.

I raised my hands, once again tracing the patterns of his tattoo, my fingers dancing across his hard abs, swirling them downward to settle on his hip, thumbs caressing the soft skin. Heat flushed through my cheeks at my own brazen behavior, but I couldn't seem to stop myself. No, I had to. Luke was waiting for me. Wasn't he?

I watched him swallow hard, and a bright edge of pleasure filled me, and I embraced it. Better than the guilt and shame I'd been feeling. It took him a second try to get words out.

"At least a few hours. Maybe more," he said, his eyes never leaving mine. I understood then. This had to be my choice.

"I'm not supposed to move?"

He shook his head, dark hair falling over his eyes. He peered out at me through the strands. I pursed my lips in thought. "And the poultice has to be on the wounds to help the healing?"

"Yes." His voice was thick, and his hands were trembling as he held my waist.

I was going to regret this moment; I knew I was. But I also knew that I wasn't completely in control of my faculties. Massive injuries, adrenaline, and lust didn't help when making decisions. So, I did what I knew my mother would want me to, to keep from throwing myself into the arms of someone I barely knew.

"I should sleep for a while then."

Bres nodded. "Here, drink a little of this, it will

help you sleep and heal." He handed me a silver flask; the cap already unscrewed. I sniffed the contents.

"What is it?" I asked, naturally suspicious.

"It's an elixir. It will help. I promise," he said.

I did as he told me to, the flavor one of honey and springtime air, lavender, and mint.

"That's really good," I said, then I hiccupped. And giggled.

It was when I tried to stand, and he attempted to stop me that I wondered at what just was in the drink. Bres took my hands.

"No, you need to lie down, Quinn."

I swayed on my feet and wondered why he was looking at me so strangely.

"I didn't think this would happen. You have too much human blood to handle this," he said, his face carefully blank, giving nothing away.

I grinned at him and put my finger to my lips, distantly realizing I was more than a little tipsy. I didn't have it in me to wonder how potent the stuff was that a single sip could have me this sauced in less than ten seconds.

Bres shook his head and lowered me back to the bed. "You should really get some sleep," he said, crouching beside the bed as he brushed his fingers across my cheek.

I blew a raspberry. "I couldn't sleep now. I want to talk."

He closed his eyes. "That's what I was afraid of, damn fairy honey."

"I'm your fairy honey?" I asked, confused at what he'd said and, to be honest, somewhat delighted by the nickname.

"No, fairy honey is what I gave you. For the human blood in you it's intoxicating beyond any alcohol and makes you talkative, blurs painful memories for a time, as well as . . ." He looked as if he was going to continue so I waved him to silence with a floppy hand.

"That's boring. I want to talk about other things," I said, then giggled and imitated his Irish accent. "Tings, I want to talk about ta tings."

He sat on the edge of the bed and sighed. "Like?"

I frowned, knowing there were things I needed to know, important things, but they slipped through my mind like water through a sieve. So, I went with the obvious.

"Do you want to be my boyfriend?"

Bres's eyes popped open wide and he choked

on a cough before answering. “Maybe, you be a saucy thing. And you do be very loyal, I like that.”

I pursed my lips and set my chin in my hands. He really was so fine to look at. All those hard angles and beautiful violet eyes made me want to lick him all over. But his other words made me think. I liked how he stood his ground. That he didn’t let anyone force him into doing something. And he was kind to me, when he had all the reasons not to be. I liked that.

Bres flushed a slow creep of red that spread up from his neck right to his hairline. I blinked at him and tipped my head, which sent the world swirling around me. I lay back on the thick blankets, laughing. “What did I say?” Were all my thoughts just popping out of my mouth?

“Yes, they are,” Bres answered. He scrubbed his face with his hands. “Now go to sleep, Quinn. You’ll feel better in a few hours and then we can get going.”

Then I remembered what I’d been thinking about. “You don’t want me to lick you all over?” I rolled onto all fours and crawled toward the end of the bed. Tears started to prickle in my eyes. “I’m not pretty enough, am I? Probably the girls you know are just like you. Stunning, long-legged, dark beauties with boobs out to here." I let out a sniffle as I tried to imagine how big the other girls' boobs would be. Bigger than my head for sure. And perfectly perky.

Bres leaned forward and lifted my chin with his finger and thumb. "No, that isn't true. You are beautiful, Quinn, though that is not what draws me to you. You have a heart in you that only makes your beauty more," His voice grew soft and I leaned into his fingers. "But this between us can't be, lovey, much as I might want it to. Or you might in this moment."

There was a little voice deep inside my mind screaming at me to control myself, that I was acting like a complete and total ding dong. But the fairy honey cut me off from all my inhibitions, worse than any whisky.

I stepped off the bed and wrapped myself around him, slipping my arms around his neck. "I changed my mind. I don't want to sleep anymore. Kiss me, Bres," I whispered, the slur in my voice thick.

He smiled up at me, his eyes dilated with a hunger I knew my own echoed. The hunger faded, replaced by a sadness so deep, my heart ached for it as he unwrapped my arms from around his neck and lifted me off his lap. "You need to sleep, right now. Let your body heal."

My bottom lip pouted, and I let go of him and tumbled back into the bed, deliberately ignoring his wry smile. "Sleep easy, Quinn. I will be close by."

17

My sleep was not dreamless. I stood on a rock balanced out in the middle of the ocean. First it tipped toward Luke who stood on the water like he was Jesus himself. Then the rock tipped me the other direction where Bres lay floating on his back in the water, violet eyes staring up at me. But it was the shriek of Ashling from out in the water that spun me around.

I jerked awake as Bres touched my shoulder.

I sat up with a groan and he dropped a jar into my hands. "Rub the poultice in good. Your wounds aren't healed up yet, they were too deep to heal this fast, but we are running out of time. We have to go." He was all business. Which was good, Ashling needed me.

I dropped my chin to my chest and slowly rubbed the poultice in. My head throbbed a little like a distant hangover, but my body did feel remarkably good—only a dull ache, for the most part. I watched Bres from the corner of my eye as he gathered his things. He was wearing a new shirt.

My priority was Ashling and Mom. That hadn't changed. And no matter how he called to me, there was no time for a romp in the sack, no matter how luscious he was. I would deal with my treacherous emotions later when lives weren't on the line.

Wearing only pants, I stood with one arm across my breasts. My shirt was shredded and saturated with blood in a pile off to the side along with my bra. "Bres, I need something to wear on top."

He had his back to me as he stood by the pit. Not bothering to turn around he said, "There are clothes to the left of the bed. Take your pick." More than bitter, his voice had a hollow sound to it. Like I'd hurt him. Should I apologize? I only remembered bits and pieces of the things I'd said when I'd been under the influence as it were.

I easily found the pile of discarded clothes and pulled out the smallest shirt in the pile. It was bloodied and had a few gashes in it, but it would do. I glanced back at Bres, who hadn't moved. Taking the largest, cleanest shirt, I used my knife to cut it into swaths. I could use it to wrap my upper body, covering the wounds. A shirt over top and voila, ready to go.

"Let me help you," Bres said, coming up beside me.

I handed him the swath of material, took a shallow breath and lifted my arms over my head, baring myself completely. Bres wrapped my wounds, starting at my waist and working his way upward, his eyes never lingering on any one spot. I wasn't sure if I was happy about that or not.

"I should have known you'd be faithful to him," Bres said, his hands working deftly, but not touching my skin at all.

I frowned and put my hand on his, stopping him. "What are you talking about?"

Bres looked down at me, his eyebrows drawn tight, and his fingers quiet under mine. "Luke, of course. I should have known you'd be faithful to him. That is the prophecy after all."

I said nothing, just stared at the far wall. I

wasn't feeling particularly faithful at the moment. Right then, all I wanted to do was burrow back into the bed with Bres and pretend that I hadn't met Luke, pretend that we weren't in a labyrinth and my sister and mom didn't have their lives on the line.

Bres shook his head and started to wrap again. "No, the two of you are meant for each other. Prophecies are never wrong, Quinn. Though I've often wished they were, have fought them my whole life, they always turn out exactly as they say they will. Forgive me for tempting you. That was unfair."

Again, I stopped him. "You just said that destiny is crap, now you're telling me it can't be changed? And nowhere did it say Luke and Quinn, XOXO, forever." Though even as I said that I could feel something settle around me like a chain around my heart.

He nodded. "I can see it in your face. You know he's meant for you too." He shook his head.

I licked my lips. "Ashling told me the prophecy." I repeated it back to him, he nodded.

"That be the one."

"But it's not plain English," I said. "The

prophecy doesn't say 'point A here, then to point B by characters C and D.'"

Bres finished wrapping me up like a mummy and tied off the tail end of it, his fingers lingering on my collarbone. With a sigh, he removed his hand from my skin and took a step back.

"The basics of it is that you will cut down evil, bring all the realms into a single one and that you and Luke are meant to be. The end." He bent and picked up a shirt, slipping it over his head.

I frowned. "Are you sure? Because as far as I can tell, I'm not much for being this chosen person. No one listens to me—I can't even rescue my own sister without being pushed out of a helicopter."

"Dragged."

"Whatever." I let out a sigh.

"Prophecies can't be bargained with, Quinn," he said, then let out an exasperated sigh of his own. He stared hard at me and I stared back. I would not drop my gaze. If anything, I lifted my chin a little in sheer defiance.

"We're probably both going to die in here." I pointed out. He blinked a couple times as if he recognized what I was saying.

"Oh, what the hell." Then he grabbed my face in his hands and kissed me.

I froze at first, then slowly wrapped my arms around him with a groan, his tongue and lips lighting a fire in my blood that made my heart pound and my body ache. I pressed my body against him, very slowly pulling my lips from his, just far enough so that I could speak.

"What was that about a prophecy?" I asked.

The corners of his lips lifted as he seemed to hold back a grin. "Prophecy, be damned."

I nodded and kissed him lightly. "That's what I thought too. Besides, if I meant anything at all to Luke, wouldn't he be here trying to save me? I think he doesn't really like me; he likes the idea of me."

Bres snorted. "He is the *Shining One,* battle general of the Tuatha. He can't come to the kingdom of the Fomorii. It would be a death sentence. So even for you, he wouldn't come here. Besides that, the council forbid him."

That was not far off from what Cora had said, that the council didn't know that Luke had come for me. I brushed a lock of his dark hair off his face, thinking of all the paths ahead of me. "What a mess this is."

He unwrapped himself from around me. "We'll figure this out once we get out of here. If we get out of here." He lifted my hand and kissed the back of it, heat trailing along with his lips.

No more was said as we left the chamber, holding hands. I didn't want to be separated from him, but as we walked rational Quinn kicked in. I didn't think I could have him and Luke too. Luke—he was waiting for me and here I was hanging onto Bres like a love-struck schoolgirl who was afraid of the dark.

The truth was, I barely knew either of them really, I was just letting my hormones get the better of me. Stupid, I was being stupid.

Ashling and mom needed me to be smart. Hell, I needed me to be smart.

Yet a part of me knew that stranger things had happened. I mean, it wasn't like I was saying I loved either of them.

So maybe I needed to cool it with both of them, at least for now. That was the smart thing. Rational Quinn agreed with me which sucked, but I made myself let go of his hand.

My fingers cooled quick without the heat of his skin against mine. Whether I believed the prophecy or not wasn't in question. The ties between me and Luke were there, and there were ties between Bres and I too.

I wasn't being fair to either of them.

"What's wrong?" Bres asked. He tried to take my hand again, but I pulled away.

"Nothing. I think I need space from both of you. Both of you make my heart pound and my brain shut off and no one needs me to be stupid right now." I said. "I . . . I'm not choosing him. But I'm not choosing you either."

"So that's how it's to be is it?" His voice was hollow. I refused to look at him, instead keeping my eyes forward.

"Yes, that's how it's going to be. Once Ashling and my mom are safe, then I'll figure this out." I knew I was doing the right thing. That I had to keep my head in the game and locked on my family.

Though I wished with all my heart it wasn't.

18

We'd been walking through the labyrinth of the Fomorii for what felt like hours, though it could have been longer or shorter. Time was hard to tell when there was no natural light, no change of the day from dawn to dusk.

My body ached from head to toe. Fatigued as I was even after the rest I'd had, the exhaustion settled on my shoulders like a weight I couldn't get rid of.

Of course, the stress on my mind was only adding to the actual physical fatigue. Any noise we made as we walked rebounded back to us, making it seem at times as if the labyrinth was crawling with other creatures when in truth, it remained silent. When I asked Bres about it he shrugged, shook his head and wouldn't answer, his eyes scanning all around us for threats.

Bres had a glow ball—at least that's what he called it—the baseball of fire I'd seen him conjure several times, that floated in front of us, lighting our way. We'd stopped for a break when I decided to push him into talking to me again.

"Will you show me how to do that now?" I asked, putting my hand out to touch the orb. It was warm, smooth like glass and very pretty, not to mention a godsend in this darkness.

"You just have to focus on what you want to make." He said.

I stretched my hand out again and thought of a glow ball. I wanted mine to be filled with blue fire. I stared at the open space above my fingers, imagined the ball, the blue fire within it. Nothing happened.

"I'm not as good at this perhaps as the prophecy thought." I snorted. "I think they've got the wrong girl."

"You have to will it into existence," Bres said. "There is no other way for me to explain it. I'm not much of a teacher. And just because you didn't do it the first time, doesn't mean you can't do it at all."

He grabbed my hands and pushed them together, the heat between us flaring instantly. I tried to ignore it. Bres didn't even seem to notice. That was good even if it stung my ego a little.

"Use them both, cup them around the area you want to create the ball. It will be easier that way," he said.

I took a shallow breath and held it, forcing all my concentration on my hands and the space between them. I needed a glowing ball, needed it to survive and so I was going to do this.

The need shifted something inside me, like a light switch turning on.

With a soft pop a small glow ball appeared over my hand, blue fire trembling within it.

"Cool," I said. He nodded and took the lead again. My little blue fire ball winked ahead of us, bobbing along beside his.

"Keep it there, if you think of it going out it will be gone," he said, "they can be finicky."

I focused my mind on the glowing blue orb. "I thought that the labyrinth was supposed to be deadly. I mean, yes I almost died but I thought it would be full of stuff like that." I asked as we walked down yet another empty tunnel.

Bres nodded. "It is. Normally it would be full of

traps and twisted Fomorii. I don't understand this. It's like they've been evacuated. Balor keeps his strongest Fomorii here, to kill invaders. Meeting one but no others is unusual."

A chill rippled through me. His strongest were usually here but now they were gone and in their place a barrier was up, meant to keep the Tuatha out. I had a feeling they weren't evacuated. In fact, I would have bet they were killed in the name of Balor's cause. I opened my mouth to test my theory on Bres.

A deep rumble beneath us set the floor to heaving, the sudden earthquake shaking the foundations of the underwater cave system. We were thrown to the floor; I lost my concentration and my glow ball went out first. Bres's was close behind mine and we were plunged back into the black of the tunnels. I gasped as the largest claw wound reopened, blood soaking through my shirt. Damn, I hadn't healed as much as I'd thought after all. Or maybe the wound was just that bad?

The rolling motion slowed, then stopped altogether.

In a matter of seconds, Bres had his glow ball back up.

"Quinn."

My head came around slowly, my ears straining. I thought I'd heard someone calling my name —and not just anyone. Ashling. I could hear her voice.

I turned to Bres. "Did you hear that?" I asked, excitement coursing through me. Had we made it all the way through the labyrinth?

He nodded, lifting his finger to his lips and doused the glowing fire ball that bobbed in front of us.

"Ash?" I whispered.

A new light flared in front of us and I had to cover my eyes. As they readjusted to the bright clear light, I could see her standing there. I reached my hand out, thinking she was indeed in the labyrinth, but it passed right through her. She was no longer in her wetsuit but wore a floor length sleeveless, burgundy dress that clung to every curve, a slit all the way up to her hip.

I asked her a question that I figured I knew the answer to already. "How are you managing this?"

"They quickened my blood," she said, her voice soft as she turned her wrist to me. A perfect set of teeth marks, human teeth, scarred her wrist. Though I knew it couldn't be, the bite looked weeks old. My hand went up to my neck where I should've had bruising and pain from being strangled by our grandfather. There was nothing to show he'd ever touched me.

Bres crouched in the shadows to my left and when I glanced at him, he shook his head, lifting his finger to his lips. Okay then, he wasn't supposed to be there?

Ashling gave me a half smile. "You need to go, Quinn. You shouldn't be here. They won't hurt me. Balor loves me."

My heart dropped as her words hit me. I scrambled to my feet. "No, you can't stay here, Ashling. They aren't the good guys—the Fomorii, they're the monsters." I winced, hoping Bres knew I didn't mean him. She couldn't mean to willingly stay here, could she?

Her image wavered. "I don't know that I have a choice. I can lead you out of the labyrinth, Quinn. Balor will allow me to do that at least. He doesn't want you here, you don't belong. And he won't hurt me or Mom. I promise you that."

Her words made no sense. She had accepted this? I didn't believe it for a second, something was very wrong.

I struggled not to yell. "Ashling, I'm not leaving

without you or Mom. You are both coming home with me."

Hope flared in her eyes. I saw it light her up then a hand clamped around her upper arm. She was yanked out of my vision.

Balor stepped forward. "You'd best take your sister's offer. There'll not be a better one." His eyes didn't match his words or his tone. While he sounded angry and his stance even showed aggression, there was a great deal of sadness in his eyes. Regret even. But that didn't make sense.

"I am going to get my family back. Whatever it takes," I said, trying not to scream at him, even as my anger built steadily.

He grunted. "Even at the cost of one of their lives? I hate to do this, but you are leaving me no choice." He snapped his fingers and a Fomorii foot soldier dragged a figure I knew all too well into view. Slight build, a massive riot of dark blond curls streaked with the odd gray strand and, though I couldn't see them, eyes the same color as Ashling's. I couldn't hold back the cry that escaped my lips.

"Mom!"

"Balor, you bastard! Let me go!" she yelled before Balor could shake her to silence.

Balor frowned down on my mother. "Darcy, you forget your place."

He turned to face me. "Her bloodline runs strong, but she isn't needed any longer. Leave now, and I will let her live. Continue in your futile search for your sister and I will end your mother's life as you know it. It is that simple. Your decision."

Horror filled me. I couldn't be the cause of our mother's death—but neither could I leave Ashling here without trying. I knew in my heart that what Ashling had said earlier was scripted. The hope that I'd seen when I'd said I was coming for them was too raw and real.

"Quinn, I know I've not always been a good mother. I know that. But Balor is right, you need to go," Mom said.

Tears pooled in my eyes. I couldn't just leave them here, I couldn't. "Please, no. He's wrong. I can get you both out. I know I can."

Balor stared at my mom and, for a brief second, I thought I saw tears form in his eyes. I frowned. What did he have to be upset about? My mom glanced up at him, an emotion—a softness—flitted across her features, gone as surely as the tear I'd thought I'd seen in Balor's eye.

"He's only right about one thing, Quinn—I'm

no longer needed." She looked over her shoulder and blew a kiss to Ashling. "I'm sorry. This chance is all I can ever give you. I just wasn't meant to be a mother. Please remember that after I'm gone."

Faster than I could believe, she snatched Balor's sword and attacked him with it. Though she wasn't doing any damage, she was keeping him at bay.

"Run, Ashling!" Mom screamed. "The labyrinth—get to Quinn!" Ashling didn't hesitate. She spun in her long dress and sprinted out of sight, for once obeying our mother without question.

The image blinked out of existence and I stared at where it had been, as if my will alone could bring it back.

"No," I whispered, putting my hand out as if I could do anything but stand helplessly by. He would kill her. I was frozen, praying he would let her go but knowing in my heart that was not going to happen.

And Ashling . . . she'd run into the labyrinth.

There was no time for my grief here. I grabbed Bres, "We have to find her."

19

"Ashling!" I screamed my sister's name, not caring that any monster might hear me. Because as it looked, there weren't many monster's left.

The blackness of the labyrinth surrounded me with only the distant sound of my own words echoed back to my ears. For just a moment I sat there, stunned by what had just happened.

Over and over I saw Balor and his sword, my mother fighting him for Ashling, and my imagination filled in the blanks. Him cutting off her head —or some horrible death blow that would leave her dying for hours, suffering alone. No, no, I couldn't think like that. I didn't know that anything had happened to her at all.

Ashling had run for the labyrinth, that much I did know.

Hands wrapped around me in the darkness and, at first, I fought them until the scent of mint poultice swallowed me up and I burrowed my head into Bres's shoulder. He squeezed me tight and I clung to him for just a moment.

"We have to find Ashling. She's in here now," I said, my voice thick with tears that I struggled to contain.

The ground began to shake again, jerking me left and right, throwing me out of Bres's hands and against a wall. Pain exploded through me, wounds ripping open, blood streaming down the side of my body.

Maybe it was some left over magic of the Fomorii, or maybe it was something extra that the monster had on its claws, but I could feel my body slowing as it fought the wounds re-opening.

"Quinn?" Bres called out to me, his glow ball flickering back to life.

"I'm here," I pushed myself to my feet. Then, as if the labyrinth had been waiting for us to lower our guards, all hell broke loose.

I was tackled from behind, the snarl of an animal right on top of me. I let out a growl of my own, rolled and flung it off as I called my knife to my hand. The smell of rot and mildew filled my senses, coating my tongue and throat. The stench of the Fomorii was overwhelming. With everything I had, I brought the blade down, again and again, but the beast didn't waver as I drove it off my back and to one side of the labyrinth.

"They be hounds of the un-dead, you can't kill them with a blade!" Bres shouted. He was farther down the tunnel now, taking his light with him. We were being separated once more.

The hound lunged at me, teeth snapping, and it was a fluke that I stumbled and spun, sidestepping the bite that would have taken my face off. Another growl behind me and I was stuck between two hounds that easily came to my waist, their decaying bodies dripping chunks of flesh. Mouths full of teeth that were as sharp as the Fomorii that had bit my leg, I had no doubt that they would tear me to pieces.

Land sharks, they were damn land sharks!

"Hold tight, Quinn, I'm coming for you," Bres yelled over the growling of the hounds. But a far more disturbing noise reached my ears over the sounds of the undead mutts.

The high-pitched scream of a girl I knew all too well.

Without any thought other than that I had to get to Ashling, to protect her, I concentrated my abilities as I swept my hands toward the hound closest to me. Blue fire ripped out of my hands uncontained by the orb. The hound burst into flame, its flesh sizzling and cracking as the beast ran from me, unable to put the fire out. Its pack mate whimpered and started to slink away. I let the hound go, the use of whatever magic I had pulled together leaving me wobbly as I ran—stumbled really—toward her screams, letting my ears guide me.

Bres, what about Bres? I stuttered to a stop. His light had blinked out at some point. Ashling screamed again and I forced myself to keep moving toward her. Bres was strong, tough. He would be okay. I had to believe that. Ashling needed me.

"I'm coming!" I rounded a corner and slipped on a patch of algae. Ashling was surrounded by hounds on all sides. I let my anger fuel me as I concentrated on the hound closest to me, directing the blue flame that erupted from my fingertips. The hound howled. It rolled into the one next to it, causing a domino effect as the flames ate at their flesh, driven by my determination that the flames would not go out.

Ashling ran between them and straight into my arms. I caught her up and held her tightly, sobs building in my chest as I clutched her to me. I had her, and for this brief moment, we were together.

"Quinn, I knew you'd find me," she whispered. "I knew you'd fight for me."

I squeezed her hard. "Always, always. Don't ever doubt it." I kissed the top of her head, the darkness around us breaking up the reunion. We had to get out of here, like *right now*. We had to get to Bres and get the hell out of this place.

It took all I had to create another orb, the last of my energy going into the floating glass ball. If another pack of hounds came on us, we were screwed.

Pulling her with me, I ran back the way we'd come. "We have to get Bres and then we can get the hell out of here," I said. Pain lanced through me as another wound broke open.

I forced myself to keep going. Not like we had much of a choice anyway.

"Quinn, you're hurt!" Ashling tried to pull me to a stop.

"No, we have to keep going. We can't stop. I don't think I can handle any more hounds and without Bres, we are pretty much sitting ducks," I said, fatigue beginning to shake me through and through.

The wounds were not healing at all now, and I had no food, no fuel since we'd been in here.

Three more turns and we still hadn't found Bres and my legs were trembling with every step. This was not good. I knew it hadn't been that far between him and Ashling—a single corner at the most.

"We're lost, aren't we?" Ashling asked, her skirts swishing along the floor the only sound besides the occasional drip of water.

"Started out lost," I said. "That's what's making this so hard. There really is no beginning or end to this, I think."

Ashling tugged me to a stop. "We can figure this out, Quinn. We're smarter than the labyrinth. Wandering in circles won't help us at all."

She was right. I let out a deep breath and sagged against the wall, one arm going around my middle. Warmth trickled down my side and I knew it was only a matter of time before I lost enough blood that I would no longer be standing.

"There's a trick to mazes," she said. "Like always take the left-hand turn, no matter what. Or go back the way you came, and you'll find where you need to go."

I smiled and let out a snort. "I think you read too much. This isn't a fairy tale, Ashling. I would love it to be that simple, but I don't think it is. I've tried going back the way Bres and I came in. It didn't work."

She shook her head. "No, I mean what if we went back to where one of the dangers was? What if the way out was just on the other side of them?"

"We still have to find Bres," I said.

Ashling went still and her eyes got a faraway look. Thirty seconds passed and then she shook herself out of it.

"They have him."

My blood seemed to freeze even as it flowed out of my wounds. "Who has him?" I knew the answer, but had to ask anyway to be sure while I prayed I was wrong.

She answered me slowly. "The Fomorii."

20

The Fomorii had Bres, which meant he was in far more danger than us at the moment despite my un-healing wounds, despite my and Ash's inability to use our powers.

"Then we have to go to the Fomorii to get him back," I said. I stood, wobbled and slumped back against the wall as the room spun and bucked, my vision dimming along with my blue orb.

"Quinn, I can help you," Ashling said. I blinked up at her, not really seeing her anymore in the poor light. I slumped further, my breaths coming in gasps.

She kept talking as she rubbed her hands together. "We all have different talents, Quinn.

Yours are strengths I'll never have, a knack for fighting that probably was helped along by the things Grandpa taught you. But he taught me too, and I think I can heal you."

She put her hands on either side of my face and a blast of heat ripped through me, followed by the frigid cold of the arctic. I gasped as the two elements warred within me, sealing shut the wounds, filling me with energy and life that had been slipping away drop by drop.

Ashling's hands slid from my face and she let out a little sigh. "That wasn't so bad was it?"

My mouth dropped open as I slid a hand over where the claws had dug into me.

The wounds were healed completely. "That was not the most comfortable of feelings, but you are amazing, Ashling!" I pulled her to me and hugged her tightly.

"Now, we can go get Bres," I said, standing on firm legs that no longer buckled beneath me.

Ashling smiled and I took her hand. But when I went to lead the way she stopped me. "I can lead us back to Balor's antechamber. That's where they will have him."

"You can?" I asked, surprised.

She nodded, the light dimming in her eyes.

"Yes, I can always find my way to the one who quickened me. It is the same for you too. Balor did this on purpose I think." We started back the way we'd come, Ashling stopping every now and then to stare off into the distance, shadows dancing over her face. It was more than a little unsettling. I wasn't sure what to make of it. I thought of Grandpa and found that indeed, there was a sense of direction, a pull to the left that I knew if I followed would take me to him.

There were no more monsters, no trap doors and no more surprises between when Ashling healed me while she led us to the antechamber. Of course, if Balor wanted her back, he would want her back in one piece and not, you know, missing a leg from a rogue Fomorii bite.

She stopped in front of a huge door at the end of a long section of the labyrinth. It stood well over twelve feet high and was made with wrought iron that had rusted so badly, it looked like dried blood. I leaned in to get a closer look. Strike that—it *was* dried blood. Ashling waved her hand at the door and it slid open as soundless as if there were no rust or blood coating its hinges.

A darkly familiar laugh echoed around us as we stepped through the doorway. The iron door slammed behind us and I pulled out my knife. As small as it was, it had seen me through a lot.

"So, my beautiful girl has returned. And you brought me a pet, Ashling, how nice. Quinn, I thought you understood that you had to leave or would die. That you were trespassing on my lands. Perhaps I did not make that clear enough. I could consider this an attack on me. In fact, I think I will."

Balor stepped forward, emerging from the shadows. He clapped his hands. Light flooded the room revealing the Fomorii that surrounded us.

"Shit," was all I managed to mutter before the Fomorii launched at us en masse. I did the only thing I could think of—I threw my hands into the air and thought of the barrier that kept me from the beach.

Safety. That was all I was thinking. Keep me and Ashling safe for a few minutes, long enough to get Bres, find our mom and get out of here.

The Fomorii hit hard, bouncing off its slick surface, snarling and clawing at it until blood ran from their lips and fingers. Sweat trickled down my face, the strain of holding even this small barrier against the Fomorii making me wonder just how long I could stand here like this.

Balor took a slow walk around the barrier I'd put up.

"Impressive. I wouldn't have thought you'd learn so quickly. *Perhaps* you are the one the Tuatha are waiting for. From what Ashling has told me of your fear of heights and water, I had many reasons to doubt it," Balor said. I saw Ashling blush out of the corner of my eye, as he continued. "I mean, really, it does seem a bit much for a scared little girl like you."

Balor lifted his hand and the mob backed off, giving him room to pace around the sanctuary I'd created. "And do you plan to stay in there forever?" He trailed his fingers along it, and I felt his touch in my soul as if it was me and not the barrier I'd created under his fingers.

"I want Bres," I said.

"I'm very aware that you *want* him. We could feel your desire all the way from the labyrinth. I wonder what the other one will think of that?" He smiled, though it didn't reach his eyes. "You Lorcan women are such teases." His violet eyes grew hard and I saw a hurt I didn't want to see. I didn't want to think about him trying to seduce Ashling, or what she might have had to do to survive. I didn't want to think about him touching her at all, but that rage gave me strength and the barrier pulsed further outward, pushing Balor backward.

"Where is he?" I growled the question as I stepped forward. The barrier moved with me and Balor's eyes widened, the Fomorii sucking in a collective breath.

Balor stepped aside with a flourish. Behind him on the floor was Bres, blood pooling around his body. Far too much blood. I glanced at Ashling, directed my thoughts at her as I had done with Cora.

Can you heal him?

Her eyes widened and her mouth dropped open. I repeated the question. She pursed her lips and gave a tight nod. *If his heart is still beating, I can.*

"You can't protect both of them; your little barrier will not be strong enough to contain all three of you," Balor said.

"Just watch me," I said. I took Ashling's hand and walked forward, pushing the barrier along the floor until we reached Bres, bringing him inside the barrier. He lay so still I couldn't tell if he was even breathing. Ashling bent to him right away, laying her hands on his face.

I thought that he would heal fast enough to make

killing him . . .maybe not impossible, but at least damn difficult.

Ashling squeezed my hand. *Grandpa should have told you his stories.*

Then she put her hands to his face, and he gasped as his body healed like mine had done. Only he didn't come around completely.

"I can't give him as much as I gave you," Ashling said. "But he will live."

"Then it's time to go," I said. I didn't really know what to do next, so I took hold of Bres's arms and started dragging him back toward the door. I could see from Balor's expression that he didn't expect me to make it out. His Fomorii were gathered as close to the barrier as they could get, their teeth snapping, claws scraping across the barrier, like nails on a chalkboard. I forced myself to focus on the barrier and put all my strength into one thought: keep out the Fomorii.

But as soon as I thought about keeping the Fomorii out, Ashling and Bres were thrown from the protection of the barrier. Balor began to laugh, the noise erupting from him in a torrent that set the room on fire with mirth. The cackling and snickering filled the antechamber as I stared at

Ashling, my mind frustrated with what I was slowly, horrifyingly beginning to understand.

Tears streamed down her cheeks and she wouldn't meet my eyes.

Balor smacked the barrier with one hand, like smacking a table when you were having a good laugh. "You didn't know? You came all the way through the labyrinth to fetch your sister, who is one of us, and you didn't know? Ha, that is a wicked twist of fate isn't it?" Balor guffawed then grabbed Ashling and pulled her to his side.

"I would no more hurt this beautiful creature than I would cut off my own arm. I even bestowed upon her the honor of being quickened by me," he said. He stared down at her with a look of fatherly love, and I knew then what my mind had been trying to tell me. What I didn't want to accept.

Balor was Ashling's father. For a brief second, I wondered if Balor was my father too. No, he'd known my father, thought him a fool, had even said I favored him in looks.

It made a twisted sort of sense. My mother had always spoken highly of the man we had known to be our father, though she would never tell us his name, because there had been *two* men.

"You hate me because of who my father is.

Because it reminds you that Darcy didn't love you most. That you came second to my father." I said, the realization popping out of my mouth before I thought better of it.

The room went so silent the distant drip of water down the walls could be heard. Not a single breath was taken as Balor stared at me, hatred filling his eyes with an intensity that made me very glad I still had the barrier up.

Balor pushed Ashling behind him and rushed me, his sword bared, a battle cry on his lips. I crouched inside the barrier and gritted my teeth. This was about to get messy.

His sword whistled through the air with a speed that I couldn't follow. I felt it strike the barrier, the echo of it rattling my bones but I held the protection from shattering. Barely. His blade bit deep and he pried it through.

"You aren't strong enough to keep me out, Tuatha!" he roared.

"Father, no!" Ashling cried out, reaching for him. He backhanded her and she stumbled away from him. Rage filled me—how dare he strike her.

I dropped the barrier and Balor lurched forward as I called my knife to my hand, slashing upward, catching the side of his neck as he fell toward me. His momentum and my strike made for an impressive wound, one that sprayed blood everywhere.

The melee that ensued was complete and total chaos. Bodies and weapons, blood and screams filled the antechamber. At one point, I was face down on the slick floor. I rolled to my back only to see a horde of Fomorii encircle me. The bone handle of my knife in my hand was a small comfort. At least I wouldn't die defenseless.

Rather than wait for them to rush me, I attacked, letting my body run on whatever instinct I had, and the training Grandpa had given me. Slashing and stabbing, I dispatched three of them within a minute and the others backed off.

"Ashling!" I yelled, over the grunting and snarling Fomorii. I could keep them at bay with my knife, but I couldn't advance. Damn it, I needed a break—something, anything. Because no matter what anyone else thought, no matter what blood ran through her veins, I wasn't leaving without my sister.

21

"STOP!" Balor roared above the snarling and growling of his people. It was if a switch had been flipped. They stopped exactly where they all were, like statues frozen in time. It would have been comical if the situation wasn't so dire. He grabbed the Fomorii closest to him by the neck, holding it tightly.

Panting, covered in Fomorii blood with the stench of rotting meat and mold filling my nostrils, I struggled to breathe. Then I stopped breathing altogether, my jaw dropping as Balor drew the life out of his vassal. The Fomorii's body went limp and then shriveled up before my eyes. The knife wound I'd given Balor healed in seconds. He dropped the husk of a body and stared hard at me, a grim look on his face.

Shifting my weight, I slid around several Fomorii who remained frozen where they were and made my way to Ashling's side. Bres was slowly sitting up, his eyes foggy with pain. He might have been hurting still, but he was alive. That was what mattered.

Balor circled the three of us, his eyes never leaving mine. I glared at him and tried to throw a barrier around the three of us. My head throbbed and my vision blurred.

"If you use all your powers up, and then try to continue using them, love, you will kill yourself," Bres said.

Balor paused and stroked his chin with his fingertips. "You two." He pointed at Bres and Ashling. "Get over here. I will not have my children side with the Tuatha."

Bres shook his head and Balor snorted. "Do it now, or I'll slaughter her on the spot."

Ashling pulled at Bres who slowly stood and leaned on her. "He will, we can still talk him down," she whispered to her brother. Damn it, her brother! Bres was her brother.

The two of them hobbled to Balor's side. I swallowed down tears. I would not succumb to hopelessness. This wasn't over yet.

"Maybe you should let your children decide what they want to do. Maybe they don't want to be a part of your world," I said, certainty filling my voice.

Balor stared at me, a glint in his eye I didn't like. "I have to give it to you, Quinn. You have fought valiantly to retrieve your family. You did say you would do anything to have her back, didn't you? Anything?"

I was shaking with exhaustion and it took me a minute to understand. He was making me an offer —do what he wanted, and I could have Ashling.

"What about our mom?" I asked.

Balor frowned at me. "You have the choice: you can either save your mother or your sister. You can't have them both."

I didn't hesitate. "Ashling."

He smiled and I was suddenly, terribly afraid of what Balor would ask of me.

"It's simple really. A challenge let's call it," he said. With a swift motion of his hands over the stone floor, the ground cracked open, splitting between us.

The stretch widened, gaping farther and

farther, water filling it until it spilled over the edges. Stone creaked and groaned, finally settling with a low rumble.

Half the Fomorii were on one side with me, the other half were with Balor, Bres, and Ashling.

"You can leave right now, with your mother, Quinn. I will give you that chance," Balor said, pointing behind me. Mom stood there, bruised, her lip split, but otherwise unharmed.

I ran to her. "Mom!" grabbing her in a hug. "I'm so sorry. I'll get us out of here."

She patted me on the cheek. "Let's go, Quinn."

"Go?" I was confused, she must not have understood. "We can't go, we have to get Ashling."

Darcy shrugged. "Leave Ashling to Balor. She doesn't belong with us. She couldn't even take the chance I gave her. I should have known she wasn't smart enough to escape."

I snatched my hands and stumbled backward, staring at her in horror. How stupid I'd been to even have thought that my mother was worth an ounce of my love. She'd cast aside Ashling?

My back to Balor, I called out. "What would you have me do? And how do I know you'll keep your word?"

Darcy's eyes narrowed, her lips tightening.

Beautiful on the outside, but she was not the person I *ever* wanted to be. I turned my back on her, faced the water and across it locked eyes with Balor.

He smiled, and though I knew we were enemies, knew that we were on opposite sides, I felt the regard he gave me. Respect. I stood a little straighter.

"Just swim across the water. That's it. Reach this side, take Ashling's hand and I will let you go. You have ten minutes, plenty of time," he said.

"Swear it," I countered. I was not going into this a fool.

He laid a hand on Ashling's shoulder and looked to Bres leaning against the wall beside him. "I swear it on the life of my children."

I too glanced at Bres. He nodded. "I don't always agree with him, but he would never hurt us."

"Quinn, you don't have to do this. We can go. Balor said that already." Darcy came up behind me, put a hand on my back.

"Your time starts now," Balor said.

I shrugged away from her. "Don't touch me. I can't even look at you right now. Why would you fight Balor for Ash if you don't care?"

"He made me angry. It was as good of an excuse as any to try and take his head. He could have kept me as his queen, but he didn't," she said, flipping her hair back like a high school drama queen.

Staring at her, I struggled with the anger that raged through me. She reached for me again. "Let's go, Quinn."

I slapped her hand off of me. "Don't touch me, Darcy. Go to wherever you want to go, but don't think I will ever forgive you for this."

She gasped and pulled away as if I'd slapped her face and not her hand. I faced the water, my body quickly shifting from anger to fear.

"You can do this, Quinn. I believe in you," Ashling called to me. I looked up to see tears streaming down her face. She knew my fears better than anyone. She knew that they were rooted not in imagination, but in reality.

"No *Jaws* theme, okay?" I said, trying to ease the tension in my shoulders and gut.

She sobbed out a laugh, nodded, and gave me a thumbs up. The water was so dark, I couldn't see anything below it, but it wasn't that far across. Forty feet at the most. A flash of movement stirred the surface. My heart jumped and my eyes tried to track what had moved. Nothing else stirred.

"Nine minutes left, Quinn," Balor said.

Shaking, I wiped my face with my hands. For Ashling. I could do this for Ashling.

I slipped out of my boots but left the rest of my clothes on. I could swim this distance in less than five minutes, easy. If I didn't have a panic attack. If nothing grabbed me. If I could get in the water.

Balor counted the minutes down.

Eight.

Seven.

Six.

If I was going to do this, it had to be now. I stepped up to the lip of the crack, stared into the waters and tried to convince myself. I even went so far as to lift my foot, only to slam it back to the ground.

"You see, Ashling? Your sister, she talks a big talk, but just like the rest of the Tuatha, there's no follow through. There is no heart in her to do the hard things," Balor said.

I lifted my eyes, shame filling me that he was right—I could say I would save her all I wanted, but I couldn't do it. I couldn't face my fears.

"Quinn," Ashling said, drawing my eyes to her.

I waited for the recrimination, maybe even the hatred that was sure to be on her face.

She smiled at me. "Quinn, you are stronger than this. You are my big sister, the one person I look up to. I know you can do this. I know you can."

Bres shifted. "She's right."

"No, she's not!" I yelled. "I've run from every monster and fear that's come my way. I'm not that strong." Shame, guilt, fear and self-loathing filled me. I was not some hero from a fairy tale.

"Three minutes," Balor said. He stared at me. His eyes, which before had shown me some regard—some respect—now mirrored my own emotions. Shame and disgust reflected back at me with perfect clarity.

Ashling started to cry. "Please, Quinn. Please try."

I walked away, my heart hammering as her sobs filled my ears. There was only one thing for me to do, only one way to escape my fears.

22

Three minutes was not going to be just enough time to swim across that gap filled with whatever monster Balor had put into it. But for my sister . . .and for me, I had to do this.

Spinning to face the open water I sprinted toward it, keeping my eyes on Ashling. The hard lip of the gap kissed my toes as I jumped, diving a good ten feet out.

Ashling, Ashling, Ashling. I thought of her missing front teeth at age eight and how I'd slipped two quarters under her pillow. Her first tumble off her bike and how she'd cried when the hydrogen peroxide was poured on her skinned knee. Holding her hand for her first day at school.

Holding her tight when her heart was broken for the first time. Watching her grow from gawky little girl into a fiery young woman with a mind of her own. My head broke the water and I was more than halfway across the gap.

Ashling was screaming at me, her face not the smile I expected, but instead a mask of horror. I didn't look where she faced. I just kept swimming. I thought of how she loved to watch Seinfeld reruns, even though she could follow the lines perfectly and could have told me every episode, she still watched it. How she'd loved her first goldfish, the one I'd bought for her, never realizing that every few weeks the "sleeping" fish was replaced with a new one. Less than ten feet away from Ashling the tips of my toes brushed across sandpaper hide that I knew all too well.

"Two minutes," Balor said. I didn't look at him, but I could hear the tone in his voice. The respect was back, and, for some reason, that was important to me.

I pushed off the sandpaper hide, grimacing as my feet were sliced up by the rough diamond-sharp skin of the shark's body, using it to propel me forward. I would not think about what lay below me.

Ashling. Her smile, laughter, tears and personality filled my mind, steadied my heart.

Five feet away, Ashling leaned over the water, reaching toward me. She urged me on. "Hurry, Quinn!" I took a stroke and reached for her, our fingertips just missing. I kicked and my feet were grabbed in powerful jaws, serrated teeth clamping down on both legs. The last thing I saw before it pulled me under was Ashling's face as she screamed my name.

The water stole my visions and I tried to hold still, tried to calm my panic. I couldn't feel my legs, which was—at the moment—a blessing.

The shark, or what I assumed was a shark, held me under the water and we floated in the stillness. It was just going to hold me until the time was up. *No.* I was a Tuatha de Daanan. This was not how it was going to end. I had magic, and I was not going to let this moment define my life again.

I only had two things that I knew I could produce. Fire, which I didn't think I could make enough of to push the shark away, and a barrier. That took a lot of energy, but I had to risk it. I gathered what was left of my strength and popped a barrier around me, pushing the shark away with an ease that surprised me.

Swimming sluggishly, I made my way to the surface, the shark repeatedly attacking the barrier. But it couldn't break through. I broke the surface of the water to Balor counting down the last seconds.

"Seven, six, five..."

I took two strokes and was at the edge. My energy gone; I was forced to let the barrier go. Ashling wrapped herself around me and pulled me out of the water.

"She beat you," she said, not looking at Balor. Placing her hands on my face, her healing power rushing through me, the bites on my legs and feet closing up as if they never were, before I could even see them.

Balor grunted. "That she did."

I stood, wobbling, flush with excitement. Ashling gripped my hand and I held tightly to her. We'd done it.

"I never doubted," she whispered. I laughed, unable to help the joy that filled me. "Well, that makes one of us."

Balor stepped forward. "You have won the challenge. You are free to go."

Ashling turned with me. "I know how to get us out from here," she said.

"Daughter," Balor called.

We stopped.

"She did not win your freedom. Quinn asked me what I would have her do. I said that she had to face this challenge, take your hand and then she would be free. There was no bargain in there for the both of you," he said.

"You lying son of a bitch!" I yelled.

"You may come and take your woman now Lugh. I believe that for this one time, I will allow you entrance to my kingdom to retrieve her. Do not let it ever be said that I don't hold to my bargains," Balor called out. Lugh, Luke. That's what Bres had called him, said that had been his name before.

A brilliant flash of light lit the room and hands grabbed me, jerking me toward that golden glow.

The Fomorii rushed us, and I clung to Ashling, making Luke drag us both. "Let her go!" he yelled at me. I shook my head and shouted back. "NO! I won't! Hang onto me, Ash!"

The choice was taken from me as Balor stepped forward and snatched Ashling from my arms as easily as if we were both children. I fought Luke, fought to get back to my sister.

The gap of water snapped shut and Darcy ran to us. I pushed her away. "No, get away! Ashling!"

"Quinn!" Ashling called, her voice cutting me to the core. Not again, this couldn't happen again.

Luke's power swirled around us and he began to pull me out of there, my mother clinging to his other arm.

"Bres! Ashling! Let me go!" I screamed as Luke's hand locked tightly onto mine. I snapped my elbow back, catching him in the chest, but he still didn't loosen his hold on me.

Bres stared at me, his eyes never leaving mine as Luke snatched me away with a clap of thunder and a light so bright, I was blinded.

And just like that, my world was once more torn apart and now I'd not only lost my sister . . .I'd lost Bres too.

23

In a swirl of water and sudden darkness I felt myself pulled upward, the depths of the ocean below us—and we were swimming hard for the surface. As I swam, I looked for Ashling and Bres. Praying that I was wrong, that they'd be with us and we'd get out of this together.

That somehow Luke had managed to do something, anything to free them.

I searched the waters around us to no avail. Hands gripped me and I looked to see Darcy struggling, her inability to hold her breath as I could quickly becoming a problem. Much as I wanted to leave her there, I knew I'd regret it. Maybe not right away, but eventually. I'd have to get her to the surface first before I went back for Ashling and Bres.

My heart sank to the ocean floor, where Ashling remained a prisoner still inside the Fomorii kingdom. We'd left them behind. Luke hadn't even tried to get them free and he'd been right there. He'd been right *there.*

Without warning, we burst upward through the surface of the water.

I pulled in a lungful of air as did the others and spun. "BRES! ASH!"

Luke dragged me forward. "Swim. We have to get out of the water NOW. They're right behind us and they won't be taking prisoners this time."

Sluggishly, turning back every few feet to look for the two that held my heart, I swam. Darcy sped ahead of us, reaching dry ground first. It wasn't until Luke circled around behind me and drove me toward the shoreline that I was forced to move at any sort of speed.

We swam to shore, the waves pushing us under, forcing us to work hard to drag our sorry asses up and out of the surf. As my toes touched the sand, I wanted to be relieved but all I felt was a twisting in my gut. We'd made it, but at what cost?

Too much, it had cost too much to get the three

of us out of there. Ashling, Bres . . . I didn't care that Bres thought his father wouldn't hurt him, he couldn't know that. Not after Bres helped us. After he helped me.

I stumbled up the beach, away from the water. I looked out on the waves, the black humping backs of the Fomorii filled the surf like a pod of oversized dolphins.

Luke grabbed me and pulled me toward a waiting helicopter where Darcy was already buckled in, her headset on.

"We have to get out of here, right now. The Fomorii are about to flood the beach," Luke said.

With a few quick movements, Luke had me buckled in too, his face tight with worry.

"You aren't even going to apologize, are you?" he asked me as the rotors started to hum.

I shook my head, my body overcome with what had just happened. I'd lost both Ashling and Bres. I had no delusions about a second chance to go after either of them

"No. I did what I thought was right." My mother was alive, though I hesitated to even call her my mother. She looked out the window, her profile in stark relief from the light shining in. "We need to drop her off somewhere. I'm not taking her with me anywhere."

Darcy turned; her eyes hard. "Ungrateful, that's what you are. Always the same with you, you always want what you can't have."

My jaw dropped and I struggled to close it, choosing instead to stare out my own window.

The helicopter rose a few feet as the first of the Fomorii pulled themselves onto the beach.

Luke shook his head and reached for my hand. His fingers were hot. They warmed my skin, which was cold with grief and a pain that I could barely swallow past. Everything I'd done had been for naught. Sure, Darcy was alive—but I'd trade her in a heartbeat for either Bres or Ashling.

"Quinn, we will have to face Bres now as an enemy. Balor won't let him go again. Ashling, too, though I know how difficult that will be for you to accept." He shook his head. "I had no idea she was his daughter. I would have told you, so that you'd know she'd be safe with him." Luke turned, and gave instructions to the pilot.

I lifted my eyes as Cora slithered out from under the seat and up onto my lap. We both ignored my mother's squeak. Apparently, she had just enough fae blood to see the snake.

"I will never see Ashling as my enemy. Never," I whispered.

Cora draped her coils around my neck. "I am sorry, Quinn. Ashling knows you loved her enough to fight for her. That will have to be sufficient for now. Sometimes that is all you can do. We don't always get a happily ever after." She paused. "But do not give up hope. That much I can tell you."

I put a hand on one of her coils and struggled not to break down, to not to give in to the gathering grief—because once I started, I didn't think I could stop. Balor had done this. The only way I could make him pay for his crimes was if I was stronger. That would be the only way I could get Ashling back. The only way I could free her and Bres from that bastard of a father.

There could be no more tears in me. I took a deep breath and slowly let it out, a plan forming in my mind.

"How can I learn to use my abilities?" I asked. If I was going to do this, I would need help, training, like Bres had said.

Luke turned to face me; his blue eyes shadowed. I wondered how he knew where to find us, how he was able to reach us just in time.

"You're right, you need training, Quinn. And

the only place you can get that through is with the council," he said, his voice just barely louder than the rotors.

The helicopter banked over the ocean, now frothing with Fomorians. Their numbers darkened the waves. I swallowed hard and thought of Bres, my heart confused at the attraction to both him and Luke. Each man held a piece of me that warmed at his touch.

I stared out at the water—the crashing waves, the brilliant blue of the sky where it touched the horizon. I had only one purpose now. I would be trained. I would find a way to lead the Tuatha and I would find a way to get Ashling back for good. There would be no more wavering with me, I would not let fear and indecision rule my life.

I thought to what Balor had done, how he'd made me face my greatest fear, thinking I would fail no doubt. Instead, he'd only shown me that I was stronger than I thought, that fear wouldn't rule me. In that, he'd done me a favor and created a new enemy.

Luke sat back beside me. "We'll drop your mother off, then we'll head for Ireland. The council will begin your training. Balor won't get away with this. I promise you that, Quinn."

I nodded and leaned my head on his shoulder. "How long will it take—the training, I mean?"

Darcy sniffed. "Your father trained for years before he was deemed able to battle the Fomorii. Years, Quinn. You don't have it in you. I've always known that. Neither of you had it in you." She sniffed again. "You and Ashling, my two greatest follies."

Her words should have stung, but I felt nothing but an emptiness where I should have been hurt. There was nothing that Darcy could do to hurt me anymore.

Luke glared at her then turned and faced me. "You are special, Quinn, it won't take that long—I think a few months, a year at the most."

A year. I blanched, thinking of the time apart from my sister, not knowing if she was being treated well, if they were hurting her. If she would think I'd given up on her.

Look after her, Bres. Please, look after her. Tell her I love her, that I'm not done fighting for her.

A distant, answering echo came back to me, the gentle Irish lilt soothing some of the pain.

Always—for you, and for my sister. Always.

UP NEXT!

Hey, so this was one of my FIRST trilogies ever written, and in 2020 I went back and edited the story for details, length, and just general improvement of the world and characters. I hope you enjoyed this story! Turn the page for the cover and link to the continuation of this world . . . .or click here—>

DARK ISLE: CELTIC LEGACY BOOK 2

SHANNON
MAYER
DARK
ISLE
A CELTIC LEGACY, BOOK TWO

ABOUT THE AUTHOR

Check out all my links to keep up to date, and my website for what's happening!

www.shannonmayer.com

Or Sign up for my newsletter

Newsletter Sign Up

Or check out my social media

Made in the USA
Monee, IL
26 March 2021